NANSHE CHRONICLES 4

STAR TRAIN TANGO

JESSIE KWAK

First edition June 2023

Cover elements by SergeyNivens, CGPitbull, and Daniel Zadorozny

Cover design by Jessie Kwak and Robert Kittilson

Edited by Kyra Freestar

www.jessiekwak.com

THERE'S MORE TO THE STORY!

... in *Artemis City Shuffle*.

Raj and Lasadi may both be down on their luck. But as a series of near misses and close calls spin their futures into a collision course, that's about to change.

Get the free Nanshe Chronicles prequel novella!
jessiekwak.com/nanshe

STAR TRAIN TANGO

NANSHE CHRONICLES 4

CHAPTER 1
JAY

Unfamiliar bass thrums through Jay Kamiya's chest, a catchy off-beat rhythm accompanied by a fast-paced duet between horn and vocals. The vocals soar and the horn chases, always a step behind as the tension of their discordant conversation builds, builds — and breaks at the chorus when vocals and horns melt together in perfect, unexpected harmony.

This shit is *good*.

It's the newest track from The Telios, a New Manilan nori group Jay first discovered back in Moie. While the rest of the crew was out playing at secret identities and cons, Jay had been prepping their ship to race the Liluri Star Run, happily getting grease under his fingernails and swapping playlists with the local dockhands. One of those, a mechanic named Su-Lin, alerted him to the new Telios track this morning.

Music is one of Jay's favorite ways to keep in touch with the people who pass through his life. It's an easy topic — every mechanic eventually gets bored of their favorites and starts sniffing for something new. Plus, it provides a constant stream of excuses to ping someone and say hello.

Nori beats were the soundtrack of Jay's time in Moie; the style reminds him a bit of the kafusa he grew up listening to, but the rhythm's faster, more erratic. The harmonies shift in surprising ways. Nori isn't background music — it demands the listener's attention, demands the body's movement.

Jay grabs his comm from its perch on the *Nanshe*'s control panel and composes a quick message to thank Su-Lin, then plays the song again from the beginning, tapping a pair of pliers against his palm in time to the opening bass lick. He settles back in to work, humming along.

His comm chimes as he undoes the latch on the environment systems control panel; a light in the lower-deck bathroom keeps shorting out and he'd like to find out why. It's too soon for Su-Lin to have gotten back to him — the *Nanshe*'s in the Pearls, too far out from the planet Indira for messages to travel so quickly.

It's also too soon for things to start going wrong on Raj's newest job, but Jay tenses for action anyway.

It's not Su-Lin, and it's not any of the *Nanshe*'s crew calling Jay for help. It's a vid from another friend made in Moie: Finley Ryan, co-pilot of Peter Fangio's racing ship, *Kalliope's Wager*. Jay'd reached out a few days ago to congratulate Finley and the rest of their crew on winning the Alusina 39. It's the last big race of the season, which probably means the *Wager* will be heading back out to Durga's Belt for a few months.

Jay swipes away the notification without playing the vid. He can watch it later. Finley's prone to rambling, and they won't need an immediate response. Jay needs to stay alert.

What are the odds he can convince Las to meet back up with Fangio's crew if they're nearby? Far better than they would have been before Raj and the others joined the crew, but Lasadi's put on a powerful armor since they landed in the Pearls three years ago. While he's sought out comrades wherever they drifted, she's diligently *avoided* making connections.

Right now, the *Nanshe* is empty. Silent but for the energetic nori beats and his own rummaging about in the environment systems controls. On the surface, it feels a lot like back when it was just him and Las, who hadn't had a presence on the ship so much as she'd haunted it, always claiming she didn't want to presume anything while it was still owned by Nico Garnet.

But it hadn't only been the fact she didn't own the *Nanshe*. Before they brought on this new crew — before *Raj* — Las had been a shell of herself. The physical trauma of their ship getting shot down, her slow recovery from the brink of death . . . that had taken its toll. But she'd also been betrayed by the man she thought loved her. And that had wounded her more deeply than the shrapnel and flames.

Jay'd fought her back from the dead physically, but he's ashamed to admit he hadn't had the endurance, on his own, to pull her back mentally. He'd been about to leave, even, before the job that brought them Raj, Ruby, and Alex. He hadn't wanted to, but he'd felt trapped in a gray current, week after week, working for Nico Garnet and watching Lasadi fade to nothing.

His ex-girlfriend Chiara had given him the way out — well, not the way out he wanted. But her invitation to move in with her gave him a starting point, a reason to express what he needed to: that he couldn't keep working for Nico Garnet, doing whatever the old Ironfall boss ordered them to do. Yet even if Lasadi hadn't agreed to take on new crew, even if she hadn't then vanished so Jay'd had to hunt her down in New Manila, Jay isn't sure he would have said yes to Chiara.

Chiara had represented a different sort of preset path. A happier one than Lasadi had been on, for sure, but Chiara was never going to leave Ironfall and join him out in the black. And he wasn't ready to settle down and raise a family on Ironfall. Wouldn't ever be, if he's honest. Ironfall never felt like home. Not like the *Nanshe* does.

Now that Jay's not completely preoccupied with keeping Lasadi together, he can do anything he wants. And what he *wants* to do is this: tinkering on the *Nanshe*, swapping musical recommendations with new people in new ports of call, and doing . . .

Well, whatever it is their little crew does now.

This is closer to what he's wanted than he's been in years. So why does he still feel so restless?

It's probably just the waiting. Jay checks his comm again, noting the rest of the crew's location beacons. Everyone where they're supposed to be, and still no emergency calls for help. Lovely if things stay that way, but Jay's not counting on it.

Still, he's got a never-ending scroll of things he needs to take care of, and it would be nice to make a dent before Las or Raj or both land this ship in chaos again. They may have paid for a major overhaul last time they were in Artemis City, but something's always breaking, which means Jay never has to worry about sitting around idle.

Once he figures out the light short in the bathroom, he's got a misfiring maneuvering thruster to sort out. It's not bad enough to be dangerous, not enough that it was high on the list before this. But Las has been complaining about it, and he'd love to have them all come home to a working ship.

His comm chimes. Now Jay's got safety goggles on, soldering two wires in a delicate procedure at an awkward angle — his dad always appreciated that Jay could fit in smaller places, with small hands for the delicate work, though Jay's built up his body over the years since he was a gangly kid in braids hiding in his father's workshop to avoid his sisters.

"Jay!"

Ruby sounds desperate, and ahead of schedule. Jay grunts and finishes connecting the wires. "You done already?"

"Negative, we've got a problem."

"Yeah, on it." Jay secures his tools and shoves his way out of the crawl space, cracking his neck as he floats his way upright. "Simple job," Raj had said. "Not a problem at all," Ruby had said. But whatever the hell is happening down there, things have gone moxed enough to call in the backup plan. "What's going on?"

"This."

Ruby patches him through to the cameras of the *Nanshe*'s shuttle, and Jay's mouth goes dry. She's got to be kidding.

"Is now a good time to say 'I told you so'?"

"Save it, love. We'll meet you at — " And then something explodes on the other end of the line.

"Ruby?" No answer. He checks his comm again. "Las?" he asks. "Raj? Alex?"

Jay shoots a look at the little mixla statue Lasadi keeps in a niche beside the control panel. One of her Coruscan opal earrings floats in the stasis field, along with a scattering of dried flower petals and a carefully folded scrap of red paper — all offerings to the little house god. Jay brushes his fingers over the mixla's head as a quick prayer, then straps himself in the co-pilot's chair and fires up the *Nanshe*'s engines. Time to save the day.

CHAPTER 2
LASADI

"I LOVE IT WHEN A JOB COMES TOGETHER," RAJ MURMURS.

He flashes Lasadi a grin and a wink, then sets off after the scar-eared man with the brutally shaved head who greeted them at the airlock. The man had introduced himself as Stubs — a nickname that could be for his short stature, his scarred ears, or the fact that two of the gloves on his environment suit have been folded over and stitched to cover for missing fingers. Or maybe it's an unfortunate surname.

Doesn't matter where he got the moniker. Stubs is now their guide to his little corner of paradise, where "recovered" ships are given makeovers and sent off to new lives with new owners who don't care where they came from. This asteroid station is close enough to Artemis to have a convenient clientele from the Pearls, but far enough out that the Pearls Federation probably doesn't sweep through much.

Location is everything, right?

Lasadi hangs back from Raj and Stubs, scanning for security and giving Ruby a chance to get a good look at everything through her lens. And also because Stubs is exuding that particular deep-ingrained reek which comes from spending too long in the black with no functional shower system.

Raj chats Stubs up as they walk, a lightness to his magbooted step and a looseness to his shoulders, like he doesn't have a care in the world. Like they're just here on legitimate — well, legitimately *illegitimate* — business and definitely not here to rob Stubs.

Lasadi would find Raj's enthusiasm charming if she wasn't so focused on making sure her crew doesn't all end up dead.

Raj had promised them a straightforward job that ticked the right boxes: helping good guys with no other recourse, taking down bad guys who were preying on good guys, and getting paid for their trouble. The plan is to talk their way into this illegal salvage op, ID a missing skiff, buy it back, then take the skiff and the evidence back to the authorities in order to get the operation shut down for good — and net a nice reward.

They'd run through scenarios until the margin of error was within her liking. Not airtight, but far better than Raj and Alex's original version of breaking in through an abandoned airlock, stealing the skiff, joyriding it back to the *Nanshe*'s cargo hold, then vanishing into the black before their marks could — hopefully — muster any sort of response.

"Got it, Cap," Ruby says through the comms. "Visuals coming in clear."

Lasadi nods faintly to affirm — Ruby will see the dip of her vision — then follows Raj and Stubs down the short access corridor leading from the personnel airlock she and Raj just passed through. The airlock has sealed behind them, a couple layers of metal and a few meters of asteroid rock the sole things between them and the vacuum of space.

The more Lasadi learns about the marvelously balanced ecosystem of Durga's Belt, the more shocked she is that anyone survives out in this tumble of asteroids for more than ten minutes.

It's not only the physical mechanics of staying alive: the oxygen, the insulation, the radiation shields, the wildly fragile walls of the habs scabbing asteroid surfaces. It's the politics. The tenuous webs of relationships that keep people *mostly* living together in harmony.

The main authority in Durga's Belt is the Pearls Federation. The Federation technically protects the shipping lanes — both those between the inner and outer planets and those within the Belt. But the Pearls are one small chain of dwarf planets in a sprawl of smaller rocks circling their system's fiery star. Stray too far away, and you're on your own.

Ultimately, pirates are kept in check not by the Federation, but by the consequences of hitting the wrong target. You never know when that little skiff you hijacked turns out to be owned by someone with a very powerful cousin. Seize the cargo from an influential business owner from Artemis City, one of Ironfall's neighborhood bosses like Nico Garnet, or a ship run by one of the many cartels or pirate groups making their homes on stations deeper in the Belt, and you won't find a safe place to go to ground.

Lasadi should know. Nico Garnet sent her and Jay on more than a few hunts, back when she was still paying off her debt to him.

The consequence of crossing the wrong businessperson or underworld boss keeps pirates wary, but the system doesn't work for everyone. If you don't have a powerful cousin — or hijackings haven't been happening often enough for the Federation to do a sweep — you have no recourse.

Like the Ahmadi family, whose son was hijacked and

marooned while on a supply run to Ironfall from their mining claim in the family's skiff. Another passing ship noticed his suit beacon and picked the kid up before he died floating in the black. Then the family put a notice with a laughably small prize up on the bounty boards, and that was all they could do. They couldn't afford another skiff, not with the supplies they'd lost to the pirates. Which meant they couldn't afford to keep working their claim, which meant they'd be giving up their autonomy for jobs in the Pearls or an indenture to one of the Arquellian corporations that swallowed and chewed up out-of-luck miners as quickly as their demolition rings swallowed up small asteroids.

No one was going to help the Ahmadi family. No one was crazy enough.

No one but Raj. And Lasadi, apparently, because here she is following him into a pirate salvage op a half-day's flight from Artemis, relying on his grifter's charm as their primary weapon.

The weird thing is, it seems to be working. So far.

Stubs leads them into a massive workshop chamber filled with ships in various states of dismantling and rebuilding. The salvager pirates have taken up inside an abandoned asteroid station, one of the many mined-out husks left scattered around the Belt. A four-seater docking arm juts out near a single passenger airlock, tucked among the hab shells on the asteroid's surface. The *Nanshe*'s shuttle, with Ruby waiting inside, is docked there. A cargo airlock built into the side of the asteroid is wide enough to allow mining skiffs and other small craft to enter, though nothing so big as a Mapalad Lowboy like the *Nanshe*.

All of the ships docked outside have legal transponders and proper paperwork — Ruby checked. Everything inside this workshop chamber is clearly suspect.

"Impressive operation," Raj says with an appropriate

amount of appreciation; Stubs had stepped back to watch their reaction when they entered the workshop.

"That's a lot of salvage," Lasadi says, not quite mustering the same level of charm Raj had — she can't stop thinking each one of these ships represents a family like the Ahmadis, driven into destitution by the theft.

"C'mon, Cap," says Ruby in her ear. "Sell it."

"Lotta operations go static out here," Stubs says. "Somebody's gotta clean them up."

Pretending to be buyers to get information to shut down the operation is risky, but it's also the real payday. This is the sort of intel the Pearls Federation will pay good money for. Even though the Ahmadi family couldn't afford much of a bounty to get their skiff back, the crew of the *Nanshe* can still make some coin off this. And hopefully get some more pirates out of the sky.

Lasadi gins up a conspiratorial smile for Stubs. "Practically a civic duty." He grins at her in agreement, and a thrill of success sparks in Lasadi's chest. Raj and Ruby were right. There is a perverse satisfaction in a good con well executed. Maybe she's cut out for this after all.

Or maybe Raj has been a bad influence on her.

He catches her eye and winks as he tucks back a strand of black hair escaped from his ponytail.

"Cap," comes Ruby's voice again. "Get him walking. We're looking for red fins."

Lasadi takes a few testing steps towards the ships, magboots clunky on the workshop's metal floor. The ships are parked against the walls haphazardly, and she can't see them all from where she's standing. "Let's see the merchandise," she says, and Stubs holds out an arm to invite her in.

"What kind of scrap are you looking for?" he asks as they walk.

"Anyone can get us scrap," Raj says. "We heard you could do something special."

Stubs bares an eyetooth in a lopsided grin. "You heard right." He leads them farther in, past a stack of dismantled thrusters and the stripped carcass of an antique beetle hauler. The trashed state of the hauler makes Lasadi's stomach lurch — it's been over a week since the Ahmadis posted their notice. What are the odds their skiff hasn't been completely cannibalized, too?

A stash of fuel cells corralled on a table beside the hauler catches Lasadi's eye and she crosses to them. Not generic cells, she notes, but lightning cartridges of the type that have been outlawed everywhere else in the Durga System because of their volatility.

Ruby whistles in her ear. "If you start shooting, watch out for those, will you?"

Lasadi nods in assent, shifting to get a better angle for Ruby. The Pearls Federation hasn't outlawed these cartridges outright, because too many people still rely on the older ships that use them — but they'll be *very* interested to know Stubs and his friends are trafficking them.

"Impressive," Lasadi says; Stubs has noticed her attention.

"Already spoken for," says Stubs. "Buyer's on their way. But we've got a few specials you might be interested in over here."

"Hold up," Ruby murmurs. "Get me a better look at the little guy on your left."

Lasadi turns to find the skiff Ruby means: an older model ChavKai Cormorant whose hull is seamed with careful but inexpert repairs. The fins are painted a jaunty red; Lasadi runs a gloved hand over the nearest with a sigh of relief. The Ahmadi family skiff, still in one piece.

"Flash, thanks," Ruby murmurs. "That's the one."

"Some of these ships are in real good shape," Lasadi says. She leans in to examine the Cormorant more closely, slipping a thumb-sized gadget out of a wrist pocket. She pats a thruster, shielding her other hand from view. "Thrusters seem new, even."

"More to the right," Ruby says; Lasadi's gloved fingers fumble for the hatch to the thruster control unit.

"We don't only do parts," Stubs says. "You looking for a solid ride — even a small fleet — and we've got you covered. Most just need a little rehab job." He grins at her. "You know. To get 'em properly running."

By "rehab job," he clearly means making changes to the cosmetics and the internal systems so they can't be traced back to the original owners. He's stopped pretending to run a simple salvage operation, which means he's either bought their con or he's not worried about getting turned in to the Federation. Interesting.

"You said 'small fleet,'" Raj says. He elbows Lasadi, eyes wide with delight, then goes to examine another nearby skiff. Stubs follows him, talking up a few of the models he has available. Lasadi lets out a sharp breath as her gloved fingers ease the catch open. She settles Ruby's snakebite kit on the now-exposed bundle of wires, then closes the hatch once more.

"Got it," Ruby says a moment later. "I'm in. Alex?"

"On it."

Alex sounds thrilled, but of course the more dangerous the job, the happier Alex seems to be. Raj, Ruby, and Lasadi had all arrived on one of the *Nanshe*'s shuttles. Alex technically had, too, but he'd been strapped to the outside and took a bit of a space walk right before they docked. Flew in under the station's radar, and has been picking his way through their security systems while Raj and Lasadi sought the skiff.

For a kid who hadn't much left the convent in all his seventeen years, Alex has taken to space crime like a pro.

"Wait for my signal," murmurs Lasadi.

"This ship's a beauty," Raj is saying to Stubs; they're

examining a late-model Bixian joyrider that *definitely* didn't belong to a poor mining family. These pirates are playing with fire. "You might be our guy. What kind of numbers are we talking about?"

"What kind of numbers do you need?" Stubs grins. "You said you had a buyer with a big appetite."

"Five to start," Raj says. "Then we'll see, depending on quality and price."

"Doable." Stubs looks pleased.

"Excellent." Raj grins at Lasadi. "We need to verify a number with our buyer, but I think we have a deal. Give us a couple minutes to make the call."

Stubs's smile sharpens. "You can make the call from here."

"Our buyer is very private."

"Then one of you can go make the call. No offense, it's just business."

"Course." Raj shrugs easy, then turns to Lasadi. "Go set it up. Stubs and I will start picking out ships."

Lasadi doesn't like it, but she doesn't argue with him. This is a complication; it doesn't have to be a problem. They'll improvise. Raj can handle himself without her.

"Pick out some good ones," she tells him, and turns to head back to the airlock.

"Wait."

Stubs's voice has gone sharp; his brow furrows as though he's listening to someone on his headset.

"Something wrong?" Raj asks.

Stubs ignores him. "I've got them right here, still," he says into his comm. He slings a pulse carbine from over his shoulder and aims it squarely at Raj's chest. "And I'll keep them here, no worries."

"What the fuck is this?" Raj says.

Stubs's answer is a glare down the barrel of his carbine.

"Cap, we've got a problem," Ruby says.

No shit.

"What's going on?" Lasadi's question is as much for Ruby as it is for Stubs.

"Another ship approaching," Ruby says. "Big one. Looking for ID now."

"Got some intel," Stubs says. "You hold tight and we'll get this all sorted out."

"Is this how you treat customers?" Raj says; Lasadi shifts her weight, ready for his sign. "Because there are a lot of other salvage operations out there we can work with. Our buyer — "

"Ain't got a thing on our current buyers," Stubs says. "Who just showed up to say you're trouble." His brow furrows again as more instructions come over his comm, then he grins. "And that they don't need all of you alive."

He swings the pulse carbine from Raj to Lasadi, pulling the trigger as he does.

CHAPTER 3
LASADI

LASADI LAUNCHES HERSELF UP AND OUT OF THE WAY, narrowly escaping the searing beam from Stubs's pulse carbine as it scorches the wall she'd been standing in front of. She catches hold of a retrofitted buttress near the ceiling as she rebounds, twisting to face Stubs.

Raj has leapt into action, too. He grabs Stubs's arm before he can take aim at Lasadi again, using his momentum to knock Stubs's magboots loose and send them both sailing farther into the workshop.

"Alex!" Lasadi yells. "Signal!"

"Copy that, Cap." Lasadi can hear the grin in the kid's voice, but she doesn't have time to be annoyed by his glee, because two of Stubs's colleagues have come charging out from the other end of the workshop to help with the scuffle.

Their attention is on Raj and Stubs, not on Lasadi floating near the ceiling; she takes aim with her sidearm and catches the first one with a slug to the thigh. They let out a strangled scream as the projectile's momentum spins them off course, a trail of blood droplets spiraling out behind them.

The other newcomer launches at Raj before Lasadi can

line up another shot, tackling Raj and knocking him loose from the stranglehold he had on Stubs. Stubs catches himself on the hull of a skiff and paws for his pulse carbine — the strap is still hooked around his elbow. He growls out a string of curses and aims at Lasadi again.

Before he can fire, a roar fills the workshop, along with a blast of heat as the engine of the red-finned Cormorant fires up. A figure grins at them from behind the Cormorant's darkened glass window, and Alex's whoop splits Lasadi's ear through the comm.

Lasadi slams her helmet shut, kicking off her perch on the ceiling and somersaulting to crash feetfirst into the pirate who's wrestling with Raj. She grabs Raj's arm — propelling them both towards the Cormorant as he fumbles to seal his own helmet — then whips a tether from her environment suit's belt and snaps it on one of the Cormorant's tether points. She hooks her arm through a ladder rung for good measure.

"Bay doors opening," Ruby says, and the pressure inside the workshop drops. Red light and sirens announce the ongoing crisis, and an emergency shield sizzles into place. It'll keep the place from completely depressurizing for a few minutes at least — but it can't stop the Cormorant.

Alex whoops again as he careens through the workshop and out the bay doors; Lasadi holds on to the rung and to Raj, her shoulder wrenching. Raj has managed to get his own tether attached, she notes with a flash of relief as Alex blasts through the sizzling shield and soars out into the black. Behind them, Stubs's eyes are wide as moons; he's dropped his pulse carbine and is scrambling for the airlock's controls.

Lasadi wrenches back around to follow the Cormorant's path. She catches a brief glimpse of Ruby tearing away in the shuttle, and . . . there. The *Nanshe*. Jay's right on time.

"Oh. Shit."

Raj is staring behind them, and Lasadi cranes her neck to find what he sees. At first she can't make out anything beyond the glare of the asteroid station's lights, but then a black shape soaks up the starry canvas beyond.

A new ship is rising behind the salvage op station, one whose silhouette Lasadi knows like she knows the *Nanshe*'s. One whose silhouette still makes appearances in her nightmares.

It's an SX Sabre, a cargo ship commissioned by the Alliance. Despite the name, Sabres are boxy and bloated, but carrying cargo instead of troops doesn't make them easy targets; Lasadi should know. Sabres are outfitted with wicked rail guns and surprisingly good aim. Lasadi's outrun her share of them, and although the *Nanshe* can't compare to the fighter she and Jay flew in the war, it's nimble enough.

Only Lasadi isn't on the *Nanshe*. She's dangling off the side of an older-gen mining skiff piloted by a teenager. The outline of the Sabre's rail gun port glows red as it slides open; less than ten seconds before it'll be ready to fire.

"Alex!" she yells. "Get us in between that ship and the *Nanshe*."

"On it, Cap."

Stubs said their buyers had arrived and ID'd the crew of the *Nanshe* — and that they didn't need them all alive. Then he fired at Lasadi, which means Raj is the one on the "don't kill" list. Hopefully that order holds — at least for a few more minutes.

Lasadi cranes her neck to look back at the Sabre as Alex swoops them in on the *Nanshe*, and while the gun ports stay red, they aren't firing. Those Sabres have nonlethal ways of taking out opponents, too, but they have to be in a little closer range. And sure enough, the Sabre's maneuvering thrusters ignite. The game's turning from a shootout into a chase — and Lasadi can handle a chase.

"Hold on tight!" Alex shouts, and Lasadi feels Raj's arm lock around her waist, holding them both out of danger as the little skiff skids into the *Nanshe*'s docking bay. Lasadi squeezes his hand as soon as they've slowed, then unhooks her tether and launches herself up the ladder to the *Nanshe*'s cockpit.

"Alex and Raj, get that skiff secured," she yells behind her. "Ruby?"

"Shuttle A is locked in." Ruby's voice is edged with panic.

Lasadi crashes into the pilot's seat beside Jay; he sits back in relief as she takes over the controls.

"Everybody strap in," Lasadi says, opening the *Nanshe*'s thrusters to full.

SX Sabres are good for a lot of things, but high-speed maneuvering through an asteroid belt isn't one of them.

Lasadi flies.

CHAPTER 4
RAJ

RAJ STAYS STRAPPED IN A CRASH CHAIR IN THE CARGO BAY EVEN after the *Nanshe* finally stops banking and soaring, letting the motion-sick roiling in his gut distract him from the sinking feeling about what comes next. Lasadi may have been able to outrun that Alliance Sabre this time, but Raj is the only one who can make sure they don't get caught in the same trap again.

What the hell was an Alliance ship doing this far into Durga's Belt? The illegal salvage op was clearly selling parts to the Alliance — and dangerous ones at that. It was Raj's bad luck they'd shown up at the same time one of the *Nanshe*'s shuttles was docked there, but it's no comfort that the Sabre hadn't specifically been looking for him. The Alliance has flagged the *Nanshe*. His father knows where he is, and what crew he's shipping with.

Raj has been aware since the beginning that his presence puts the rest of the *Nanshe*'s crew in danger; he just thought he had a few more months before it came to a head.

"We've lost them," Lasadi says through the comms a moment later. "Everyone all right?"

A chorus of yeses; Raj doesn't join in.

"Cap?" Ruby says. "That Alliance ship, only. I intercepted their message to the pirates."

A pause, a touch too long; Lasadi can guess as well as Raj who the Alliance ship was after. "Queue it up," she finally says. "We'll meet you all in the cargo bay."

Raj unstraps himself as his crewmates gather. Alex pops out of the recovered skiff, a sheen of sweat glowing on his dark, freckled brow. He grins and slaps a hand on the skiff's side like he's ready to take it for another joyride. Ruby emerges from the *Nanshe*'s Shuttle A airlock, worrying her lip, red-lacquered nails tapping nervously on the back of her tablet. Jay floats down the ladder from the upper decks, unruffled as always. He's the only one of them not in an environment suit, his sleeves rolled up over taut biceps, shag of black hair drifting into his eyes as he returns Alex's smile.

Lasadi follows Jay down, expression drawn, smoky brown eyes unreadable. A muscle jumps in her cheek when she meets Raj's gaze.

Raj gets slowly to his feet. "Play it, Ruby."

Ruby taps her tablet, and an Indiran Alliance commander's cold, dispassionate Arquellian drawl fills the cargo bay.

"We've identified the shuttle docked at your station, and we believe you're dealing with a wanted fugitive. I'm sending an image now. Please detain Raj Demetriou, we need him alive. Deal with the rest as you will."

Deal with the rest as you will.

Raj breathes deep, his previous unease replaced by icy certainty. He doesn't recognize this particular commander, but he does recognize the casual way she declares everyone on the *Nanshe* — except for him — collateral damage. It's no comfort to find out the bounty on his head has apparently changed to capture instead of kill. Not when the

Alliance knows who he's shipping with and considers them disposable.

His father doesn't give a shit who he hurts so long as he can bring his son back home in chains. Raj can't stay here.

He opens his mouth to tell them his decision, but Alex pipes up before he can speak.

"How did they know Raj is on this ship?" Alex asks. "And where to find us?"

"They didn't know where to find us," Lasadi answers. Anger smolders in Lasadi's eyes, and Raj doesn't blame her. He's furious with himself, too. "We were wrong place, wrong time, and they ID'd our shuttle. Ruby, can we fix that?"

"Jay and I will chat on it." Ruby nudges Jay with her shoulder. "Won't we, love."

Jay nods. "I've got a few ideas."

"And the bounties?" Lasadi asks. "I thought that was taken care of."

Raj clears his throat. "The bounties — "

"I'll do another sweep," Ruby cuts in, ignoring him. "But I've got a crawler on the boards, so I should have heard if there was a new one. This might be internal to the Alliance, only."

"Can you find out?"

"Course, Cap. You're talking to Ruby Quiñones, aren't you."

"Then do it. Jay, tell me we lost the Sabre for good."

"Yep. They sent out a couple of their scouts, but we were long gone by then."

"Captain," Raj says, but Lasadi ignores him.

"And they had a shipment to pick up." Lasadi's eyes narrow in thought. "Those lightning cartridges. Why would an Alliance Sabre be so far out from Indira to pick up something so dangerous?"

"Captain," Raj says again.

Jay scrubs a hand over his jaw. "I don't like that at all. I'll see if I can find any intel."

"Lasadi."

In the sudden silence, Lasadi's name on Raj's lips sounds like a shout. Four pairs of eyes finally turn his way, and a cool, hard weight flips over in his stomach.

"I appreciate you all trying to solve this problem, but no one's addressing the real issue," he says calmly. "If the Alliance knows I'm on this ship and is willing to kill anyone around to get to me, then none of you are safe. I'm putting you in danger."

"You're not going anywhere," Lasadi says sharply. "End of discussion."

Ruby's shaking her head. "Cap's right, love. We have plenty of options before 'maroon Raj on a deserted asteroid' becomes the plan."

"You don't have to maroon me," Raj snaps, frustrated. "Drop me off at the nearest port."

"Look, man," Jay says with a shrug. "If you've pissed Las and Ruby off to where they don't want you on the crew, you're probably being marooned on an asteroid."

"That's the best-case scenario," Alex agrees gravely.

Ruby lifts an eyebrow at her little brother. "Goes for you, too, doesn't it."

"Hey!" Alex raises his hands. "Raj is the one in trouble. I didn't do anything!"

"That I know about, only."

"No one's getting marooned," says Lasadi. She sounds exhausted, but a smile's tugging at the corner of her mouth, and when she meets Raj's gaze this time, her expression is soft. She *was* angry before, he realizes, just not at him. Captain Lasadi Cazinho has her own reasons to hate the Alliance, and this encounter brought her protective fury roaring to the surface.

Thank the gods they're not fighting on opposite sides of a war anymore.

Lasadi lifts her chin, and the little crew comes to attention. "Ruby and Jay, come up with a plan to disguise the *Nanshe*. We should have done that anyway — too many people out here know this ship used to be Nico Garnet's. Alex, tell the Ahmadis we have their skiff, and we'll be in touch about returning it once we have a safe way to do so. Raj, write up everything we learned about that salvage op and submit it to your contact in the Federation." She pauses. "Leave out the part about one of their buyers being the Alliance, for now."

Murmurs of "Yes, Cap" around the group as everyone receives their assignments, and Lasadi turns to hold Raj's gaze. He takes a deep breath; he still owes them all an apology.

"If not you, they might have been looking for me," says Lasadi softly, stilling his apology on his tongue. "Or Jay. We're fugitives, too."

"Maybe," Raj says. "Except everyone thinks you're dead."

Ruby squeezes his shoulder. "They could have been looking for me."

"Or me!" Alex chimes in; Jay laughs and elbows the kid.

"You're not wanted anywhere."

"Yet!"

"Don't rush it." Lasadi smiles at Raj, and a complicated warm glow kindles in his chest. Her hand flexes at her side, and he gets the impression she might have reached for his hand if it weren't for the small crowd gathered around them. They've stolen a few moments for conversation in the weeks since Sapis Station, but the *Nanshe* is a small ship and there hasn't been any privacy.

Another woman might not have cared, but Lasadi's navigating her responsibility to this crew as well as old demons that have made her wary of opening up. Raj wouldn't say he's become an expert at reading her since their paths first collided, but he's spent hours studying that face. Surreptitiously at first, openly since she kissed him on Sapis Station.

He returns her smile, lightness flooding through him. His crew has his back, and he'll soak up every offered ray of Lasadi Cazinho's sun until she's ready to give him more. Not knowing if she would return his affection had been an impossible weight. Now, knowing the answer is yes, he's content to go as slow as she needs.

"Next matter of business," she says to him. "We lost our Alliance tail back at the salvage op. Are you worried we'll bring trouble to your friends Vash and Gracie if we still head there as scheduled?"

"No," Raj says. "If you say we're clear, we're good. No one knows my connection with them — and they have plenty of precautions at the Emporium."

"Okay." Lasadi straightens her shoulders. "Next stop, the Traveler's Emporium."

When Lasadi calls him to the bridge a few hours later, Raj breaks into a smile at the view filling the screen. It never gets old, and lately it's been feeling more and more like home.

The Traveler's Emporium is a series of asteroids bound together artistically from biggest to smallest, the way Raj's mother used to stack river rocks on quiet picnic afternoons at the stream — mother-son outings — before his father declared such afternoons wastes of time and his mother's laughter stopped coming so easy. Like his mother's stone cairns had been, the Emporium is a labor of love. Unlike them, it's been designed to withstand centuries.

The Traveler's Emporium is an awkward distance from Artemis and Dima, just past the smallest dwarf planet in the Pearls, Nerrivik. Awkward in that if you're headed out for a long journey, you probably secured your supplies and fuel before leaving the Pearls. If you're on your way *to* the Pearls, you'll probably stay the course and skip the lost time and burn of an extra stop.

Which means those strangers who do end up at the Emporium are a motley bunch: poor planners in need of last-minute supplies, drifters in the know who are willing to pay a bit more for supplies to avoid heading all the way into the Pearls, and the curious who are drawn in by the Emporium's vibrant chaos and playful signage.

Because whether or not a belt drifter has ever stopped at the Emporium, they've definitely noticed it.

The Emporium's stacked asteroids are a riot of color and light from tip to tail. A holographic neon sign spins in a slow dance off the smallest asteroid, lazily blinking letters that read, *Stop at the Traveler's Emporium!*

"I'm still not convinced this place isn't owned by serial killers," Lasadi says.

"Vash and Gracie will be flattered," Raj answers. He settles into the co-pilot's seat of the *Nanshe* while Lasadi guides them closer, watching Lasadi's face as she takes it all in. After the neon sign, the most noticeable part is Gracie's sculptures, tethered at random intervals around the station. A racing dart she painted neon pink and cut into careful slices, then mounted on a cable to create the illusion of a ship that's come apart midflight. A fantastical bird constructed of scrap metal, with heat-reactive paneling that shifts in hue as it spins, rippling rainbow shades where the bird's feathers would be. And, of course, the countless scrap spirals and arcing wings, Gracie's signature pieces.

Lasadi whistles low. "There's a wing like that in Artemis City's passenger terminal."

"It's Gracie's," Raj confirms. "One of her biggest commissions, but she's sold pieces throughout the system. Arquelle, Bulari, Bixia . . ."

"So they don't really need the tourist business," Lasadi says. "I've always wondered who would be crazy enough to stop here."

"Most of their regular customers are other inventors and artists, antiquities dealers — they have an odd assortment of friends."

Lasadi slides him a smile. "Arquellian grifters?"

He smiles back. "And hopefully soon a couple of Coruscan freedom fighters and Artemisian scoundrels."

"Seems lonely," Lasadi says after a moment. "And dangerous, out here on their own."

"Vash used to do work for a lot of the old Ironfall bosses," Raj says. "She still has a lot of powerful friends in the Pearls underworld, and Gracie has a lot of rich patrons. People know not to mess with them." He lifts a hand to point. "Not to mention their security is tight. You see those crenellations on the chicken?"

"I think it's a parrot," says Lasadi.

"Agree to disagree."

Lasadi leans in to study the bird sculpture more closely. "You're right. Those cannons would take you out in a heartbeat if they didn't want you here."

"And they have state-of-the-art shielding," Raj adds. "Once we're inside the docking bay, not even the Alliance's scanners will be able to pick up a trace of the *Nanshe*."

"More evidence serial killers live here," says Lasadi, laughing. "Where have you brought us?"

"Home." The word slips out unexpectedly; Raj clears his throat to cover his surprise, ignores Lasadi's curious look. "The bay doors are there," Raj says, pointing to the widest end of the stack of asteroids. "If you're done admiring sculptures and ready to get serial-murdered by my friends."

"Beats flying exposed like this," Lasadi says. "The sooner we can disguise the *Nanshe*, the better I'll feel."

The reason for that cuts through him once more. "Las," he says, and this time she doesn't try to shut down his apology. "I'll do everything I can to protect this crew."

"I know," she says quietly. "And we'll do everything we can to protect you."

Her hand slips warm into his. She shifts, lips parting as she pulls him closer.

And a connection request flashes on the *Nanshe*'s controls. Lasadi smiles ruefully, the moment broken as Gracie's voice comes through the speakers.

"Traveler's Emporium to *Nanshe*. Glad you're here, I hope the trip was smooth."

Lasadi nods to Raj, who leans forward to hit the comm switch. "Glad to be here, Gracie. We might have had a little adventure on the way, but we didn't bring any trouble with."

"Famous last words." But he can hear the smile in the older woman's voice. "Opening the doors now."

Lasadi releases Raj's hand with a squeeze and turns back to the controls. She orients the *Nanshe* belly-down to the bay doors, then lowers the ship in and follows the guidance lights to an open dock. A mild jolt shudders through the ship as the clamps secure the *Nanshe*, followed by the pull of artificial gravity and a nervous excitement curling in Raj's chest. Vash and Gracie are the closest thing Raj has to family anymore — the closest thing he *had* to family until he connected with this little crew. His two worlds are about to collide.

Gracie is waiting for them in the docking bay when the *Nanshe*'s cargo door opens, beautiful as ever with her warm brown skin, broad grin, and smiling eyes. Today her black hair is pulled back to showcase swaths of silver at the temples, the strands glittering through her long braid. Enormous earrings shaped like jungle leaves clatter when she steps forward to give him a bear hug.

Her embrace is strong, even though she barely comes up to his shoulder. She hugs the rest of the crew as he introduces them, trying not to give any special weight to Lasadi. And failing, given the way Gracie's eyes sparkle at him over Lasadi's shoulder when she brings the other woman in for her greeting hug.

"Hope we didn't keep you up too late," Lasadi says. Local time at the station is well after dinner; they'd hurried so as not to arrive in the middle of the station's night when the women would be asleep and they'd have to spend the night in orbit. Which wouldn't normally be a problem, but after the encounter with the Alliance, they were all keen to get out of sight as quickly as possible.

Gracie waves a hand. "No problem. I'm a night owl anyway, but Vash will be jealous I got to meet you all first. All that nonsense about the early bird getting the worm, it's the night owl who gets the gossip."

There's the faintest emphasis on the last word, a twitch of a smile Gracie gives Raj. She's seen right through his attempts to downplay how meaningful this crew has been for him, and its captain in particular.

"That said, I'm sure you're all tired," Gracie says. "And Vash will kill me if I talk your ears off without her. Let me show you to your rooms — with your permission, Captain?"

"Of course." Lasadi holds out a hand. "You all go ahead; I'll stay with the ship."

Gracie opens her mouth as though to argue, but Jay cuts in. "You can't talk her out of it," he says. "I wouldn't try."

"What, and miss my chance to have some peace and quiet?" Lasadi smiles. "Anyway, after our adventure, there are a few things I need to check before I'm ready to call it a night."

"Did you need a hand?" Raj asks, aiming for nonchalant.

And maybe he's hit nonchalant too well, because at first Lasadi shakes her head. "No, that's fine, I — " She cuts herself off, meets his gaze. She clears her throat. "Actually, yes. If you don't mind."

"Course, Captain." Raj ignores the creeping heat under his collar and wills the others to do the same. But it's far too wild a hope for that exchange to have gone under the radar. Ruby rolls her eyes at him, Jay gives them both a wry smile. Alex begins furiously studying one of Gracie's sculptures, pretending he has no idea what's going on.

Gracie gives Raj a wink. "You know your own way," she says. Then turns to the others. "After me!"

Raj follows Lasadi back into the *Nanshe*, closing the bay door behind them.

CHAPTER 5
LASADI

NEITHER OF THEM SPEAK UNTIL THE ECHO OF VOICES AND footsteps has gone, swallowed up in the stairwell that must spiral down through the core of the station.

Partly because Lasadi has no idea what to say next.

It's not that she hasn't been *alone* with Raj. They've spent long hours together since Sapis, since she finally admitted she wanted more out of their relationship. But there's nowhere truly private on the *Nanshe* except their individual cabins, and it had seemed far too awkward to suggest such a thing while the rest of the crew was on board.

Ridiculous. Like she was a teenager living with her grandmother and younger siblings and worried about bringing a boy home.

To be fair, if she'd ever had much game with men, it's extremely rusty. She hasn't seen anyone since Anton; almost dying and then working for Nico Garnet will put a damper on a person's love life, and she hadn't been able to go through with any of the casual flings that presented themselves over the past few years.

She'd started to wonder if maybe she didn't need sex.

Not everyone does — maybe her physical attraction to Anton had been an extension of her enchantment with his ideas, maybe she'd been young and experimenting. As the idea took hold, she'd almost been relieved at the promise of a nice platonic future; one where she'd never have to explain her scars.

Then Raj walked into her life, and from the first moment their eyes met, he'd lit up every fiber of her body.

She's stopped fighting it. That doesn't mean she knows what to do next.

Raj has closed the *Nanshe*'s bay door; now he turns to face her, shoulder blades propped against the wall. Hands in pockets, like he doesn't have a care in the world. He doesn't, probably. He's not the one doing desperate calculus around lighting options and the timing of clothing removal.

"I normally have a plan for this," Raj finally says. He cracks a knuckle, doesn't seem to notice the gesture. Maybe he's not so relaxed after all.

"A plan?" Lasadi laughs. "Do you do a lot of 'this'?"

"Not since I've been on the run." Raj's smile becomes wry. "I'm a little out of practice."

"Same." Lasadi lets out a breath and steps forward, hand out; he twines his fingers with hers and draws her knuckles to his lips, tracing fire over each joint. "What's your usual plan?"

"It's classic. I'd take you out on the town. Dinner at a nice restaurant in Artemis City, then a walk in a park. We'd talk, do some people-watching. Then maybe we go back to mine for a nightcap."

Lasadi laughs. "Back to your single-wide bunk, you mean?"

"I'm a man of simple means, but I do know how to show a lady a good time." Raj grazes the pad of his thumb over her knuckles. "Unless you really do need help around the ship."

"The ship can wait." Lasadi's a handsbreadth away now, so close she can feel his heat. Raj still hasn't moved. "Your single-wide bunk sounds enticing, but I can get us into the captain's quarters."

"Are they nice?" Raj shifts forward, lips hovering above hers.

"Do you want a tour?" Lasadi's free hand falls to his hip, traces the line of his waistband before her fingers curl in; she savors his sharp breath as she tugs him closer, closer.

When their lips meet she loses her breath. He smells like sea salt and citrus, tastes clean and bright and warm. His hair is down, loose black curls around his ears, and a lock falls free to brush her cheek — she smooths it back, letting her fingers tangle in the thick strands. His left hand flattens against the small of her back to draw her in closer, his right slides up from her hip, over the hollow of her abdomen, so close to that ridge of scar tissue —

Raj breaks off the kiss, concern in his dark eyes. "I have no expectations," he says; he's created space between them but hasn't quite pushed her away. "If you're not comfortable — "

Olds, she's gone tense as a tethering cable at his wandering hands, that wild heartbeat in her throat equal parts arousal at his touch and apprehension about what happens next: buttons undone, boots tumbling into corners, shirts discarded . . . and Raj's inevitable look of horror.

It doesn't have to be that way, she tells herself. It *won't* be that way, not with Raj.

"It's fine." The words are meant for them both. "I want this." And she wills herself to relax into his touch again, burying her nose against his neck to savor the tender skin there, laughing when he lifts her and spins, settling her against the ladder to the upper deck with her legs wrapped around his waist — a pose which doesn't last long since the metal rungs are designed for utility, not comfort. She breaks free, laughing, and pulls herself up to the crew deck.

She has her boots off by the time he joins her, and his jacket off by the time they stumble past the medbay and into the kitchen; his strong fingers fumble for the tucked hem of her shirt but she steers them away with a jolt of nerves she tells herself is excitement. This will work. She'll make this work.

The Mapalad Lowboy design is intended for longer hauls and favored by families because the two forward cabins are relatively spacious and have room for double beds. Ruby's is starboard, a riot of color and discarded clothing; Lasadi's is port, and she's still done little to decorate, even since taking over ownership of the *Nanshe*.

Not that she or Raj are paying attention to the decor. The backs of Lasadi's thighs hit the edge of her bed and she falls with a laugh — her clumsiness a combination of gravity after the weeks in transit and the innate awkwardness of two bodies navigating each other and space. Raj laughs, too, and steps away to pull off his shirt.

He turns back to catch her ogling, and Lasadi almost apologizes by reflex. But they're alone, he's enjoying the attention, and Lasadi gives herself permission to truly appreciate his toned shoulders and smooth, planed torso. She's caught glimpses — the *Nanshe*'s quarters are tight, and no one but her is particularly modest. But right now, as he carefully lays aside his shirt, as he slowly undoes the top button of his trousers and lets them slide down his hips, the show is meant entirely for her.

Lasadi's heart kicks up another notch as he joins her on top of the covers, the length of his body sliding alongside hers. This time his kiss is hungry but patient, his fingers certain as he slowly undoes the top button of her shirt, then the next.

A spike of adrenaline; she catches his hand in hers and breaks off the kiss, trying for an *Everything's fine* smile. "Let me get the light," she says, reaching past him for the bedside switch.

"Las."

Raj props himself up on one arm beside her, opening a gap between their bodies. It's scant, but enough for the ship's cooler air to creep in where his heat used to be. Lasadi opens her mouth to explain — to tell him everything's fine, to insist on the light — but Raj lets his hand fall to her left hip. He sweeps his thumb up to brush the ridge of scar tissue in the hollow of her abdomen, leaving a trail of fire in its wake.

"I know you were hurt," he says gently. "I've felt this scar before, and I'm going to see it sooner or later. Unless you were thinking this is a one-time thing."

"I don't want it to be."

He knows — or, he thinks he knows. She told him she and Jay had been shot down at the Battle of Tannis, and Jay probably gave him more details. Raj might even have heard about the months she spent in Nico Garnet's regen tanks and hospital rooms, but still. Whatever he's braced himself for, this will be worse than he imagined.

Lasadi closes her eyes for a heartbeat, then begins to work the remaining buttons of her shirt. His gaze traces the path with a playful smile as she reveals delicate blue lace — an impulse purchase last time they were in Artemis City, even while she'd been planning to shut Raj's advances down — and a swath of pale stomach. With a deep, shaky breath, she tugs the tucked-in hem free and lets her shirt fall open all the way.

She keeps her eyes on his face as his smile vanishes; she knows what he sees.

The starburst of burn scars starts on her ribs, swirling in mottled shades from glossy ivory to nearly scarlet. The old burns sweep up to trace her collarbone and shoulder, down over the curve of her waist to feather over her hip before disappearing beneath her waistband. They're not the only scars on her body, but they're the most noticeable — along with the scar he'd felt before, the jagged ridge running from below her ribcage to her hipbone.

"Gods, Las," he breathes.

"The scars cover most of my thigh." She lifts her chin defiantly, telling herself to just get it over with and face the rejection she knows is coming. "And a lot of my back. I know, it's — "

"Does it still hurt?" he asks, and she curses herself for thinking they could have had a normal night without the trauma of her past taking center stage. Even with the lights out he would have noticed. If she hadn't been too afraid to bring it up earlier, maybe they would have had a chance, but revealing her scars this way? Can she blame him for being shocked?

Lasadi starts to sit up, but Raj presses a kiss to her collarbone and slides his hand from her waist, brushing lightly over the livid scar on her abdomen, smoothing over her ribs, thumb teasing over blue lace. Lasadi gasps.

"That's not what I meant," he murmurs into her neck. "I was trying to ask, do I need to be careful?"

"No," Lasadi says, breath shaky. "It doesn't still hurt."

"Good." His lips find the warm skin below her ear and she shivers against him. "Tell me what you want."

"This." She's not sure what else to say; she hadn't had the capacity to imagine they'd get this far, and she has no idea what to hope for next. "You."

His response is a nip to her earlobe that sends lightning coursing through her body, and she slowly forces herself to relax as his hands and lips explore. It gets easier with every kiss, every touch. He doesn't pay her scars any special attention — but he also doesn't avoid them. He treats her as though she were whole, and for a moment she can almost forget she's not.

Her entire body is ablaze by the time he finally, lazily, snaps free the top button of her trousers. He plants a kiss in the hollow above her scarred hipbone, then eases them down over her hips.

"We still good?" he murmurs into her thigh, and she gasps assent. Raj smiles up at her. "You can still turn off the light if you want. But I bet you'll enjoy the view as much as I will."

The light stays on.

CHAPTER 6
JAY

"AND THE APPLES, MAN — YOU CAN EAT THEM FRESH OFF THE vine or whatever they grow on. I've never tasted anything so good in my life. They have like a hundred different kinds — did you know that? There are *so many* kinds of apples in Alusina, it's mind-blowing. And the hills, green for days. I don't understand why anyone on New Sarjun lives in Bulari when Alusina is an option. Bulari's a total shithole, everybody knows that. Anyway, for the apples alone, you *have* to talk Cazinho into trying her hand at the 39 next year, you'd both love it. Okay. Right. I've probably talked your ear off long enough. It was good hearing from you, friend. Keep in touch, and stay safe out there."

Jay swipes Finley Ryan's vid closed with a laugh. What had started as a play-by-play of Peter Fangio's winning Alusina 39 run had ended with a five-minute ode to fresh produce, Finley's face lighting up even more with every new fruit they described eating.

"Talk Cazinho into trying her hand at the 39 next year," they'd said. Maybe someday the crew of the *Nanshe* will be in a place where they can spend a season racing like Fangio and his crew on the *Kalliope's Wager*, but Jay's not sure when that day might come. He and Las had snuck under the noses of everyone but Fangio's crew during the Liluri Star Run, but they can't take that risk again — especially now that they know the Alliance has a bead on Raj being on the *Nanshe*.

Jay slips into the hallway to find the bathroom, then hesitates before returning to his room. He should get some shut-eye, but he's not tired.

He's never had much trouble sleeping, even in a new timezone. The trick is to start thinking in the new timezone long before you arrive, and banish all thoughts of what the past timezone was. Maybe the last meal they ate on the *Nanshe* was technically lunch, but he'll tell his brain it was dinner and that now it's time to bunk down.

So it's not the timezone, and it's not the rooms — they're very nice. Jay had been expecting a wall of crew bunks like you so often find in old asteroid mines turned full-time living. But Jay's room has a decent double bed, wash station, and even a folding stand to hold his duffel. Ruby's and Alex's rooms were similar, and there were another dozen identical doors down the hallway. Gracie and Vash could run a hotel service if they cared to.

Jay should sleep. But standing in the hallway, he knows he's far too wired to rest.

He's not the only one still awake. He can hear Ruby's voice — sounds like she's recording a vid call, probably to Kitty — and the annoying little chime of the new game Alex has gotten hooked on. And, from above, unfamiliar music.

Gracie had said she was a night owl, and she'd been working when they arrived. Had she been killing time, waiting up for them? Or is she back in her workshop, wrapped up in a project? Jay heads up the stairs to find out.

The Traveler's Emporium is set up like a spindle, each asteroid hollowed out and stacked on each other, rooms carved around a central core, the space getting smaller and smaller the farther along you went in the chain of asteroids.

They'd arrived in the dock level, with its large bay doors and parking area. Gracie's workshop is below, sharing the level with the Emporium's public storefront. Vash and Gracie's living space is in the level below, with the guest rooms below that. The ladder shaft then continues down to what Gracie had told them are maintenance levels and storage.

Jay climbs — there's an open-air lift platform, they'd ridden it down, but it was clunky and noisy and Jay doesn't bother with it, not when there is a perfectly serviceable set of stairs spiraling around the outside of the shaft. He climbs past Vash and Gracie's living quarters, his suspicions about where the music is coming from confirmed as he gets closer to Gracie's workshop.

The storefront half of this level is dark, but the lights are still on in the workshop, giving Jay a tantalizing glimpse of her many projects. She may have become famous for her sculptures, but there's plenty of machinery in various stages of dismantlement that Jay would love to poke around at.

Gracie's there, like he suspected, humming quietly along with her music while she works. Jay makes a decent amount of noise dismounting from the stairs, not wanting to startle her. The older woman is crouched at the base of a glowing two-meter metal fang balanced on its point. The fang is surrounded by rings of varying widths, each made from a different type of material. She glances over her shoulder at Jay, then finishes taking a measurement and stands. She pushes her goggles up on her forehead.

"Couldn't sleep?" she asks.

"I heard music," Jay says. "Hope I'm not bothering you."

"Not at all. Normally Raj is the night owl with me when

he gets in, but seems he's more interested in chatting up your captain than this old woman tonight." Her gaze flicks mischievously to the ceiling, then she crouches down again. "Be an angel and give me a hand?"

"What are we working on?" Jay asks, letting Gracie direct his hands to hold things in place, face turned away as she welds.

"A commission — one of the hubs in Ironfall had some extra budget for beautification and decided an art installation was the thing. This'll go in the market at Selena's Ante. You've been there?"

"Yes, ma'am. My girl used to live near there." Jay shifts his fingertips away from sparks. "Or, she still lives there."

"She's not your girl anymore."

"Yep."

"Vashti and I tried the long-distance thing for a while when we first met. I hated it."

"Yeah? How'd you two meet?"

Jay doesn't want to talk about Chiara; it's not the loss of the relationship that still digs at him, it's the fact he knows he broke her heart. He can't stop remembering the pain on her face when he told her he was going after Lasadi. He'd known he wasn't going to stay, not in the way Chiara wanted. But he would have liked to end things better.

Instead, he'd been selfish. He'd tried to have the best of both worlds: someone to come home to who enjoyed hearing about his adventures, and also a life of adventures which kept taking him away from that someone. Chiara never would have joined him on the *Nanshe*, and he couldn't settle down in Ironfall. It had been an impossible conundrum then, and one he still can't see a way out of now.

Gracie shoots him the briefest glance, like she knows he's changing the subject, but she doesn't press.

"My family worked mining claims when I was little," she says, lifting another piece into position. Jay leans forward to hold it in place while she welds another line. "Before they joined a collective that owned one of those big ore-processing plants. I remember thinking it was amazing as a kid, watching them harness small asteroids and feed them into the beast. Swap me places." Jay does, and Gracie keeps working. "We had one of the most valuable namidium mines in the Belt."

Jay lets out a low whistle. "So we have your collective to thank for the *Nanshe*'s fancy booster upgrades."

"You and the rest of the system," Gracie says with a faint smile. "Once I was old enough to have a real job with the collective, I started doing supply runs to the Pearls. Vash grew up in Ironfall, and we met there."

"The long-distance thing."

Gracie laughs. "Like I said, I hated it. I had to keep going back to the collective with supplies, but eventually I convinced her to join up with me."

"How'd she like being away from Ironfall?" he asks, ignoring the pang in his heart.

"She loved it. You'll meet her tomorrow — Vashti has always been adventurous." She finishes another expert line, then leans back with a sharp crack in her hip and a wince. "We worked here and there for a bit, then finally decided to sell our shares in the collective and start building this place."

"When did you know it was time to settle down?" Jay asks.

"When we both had amassed too much junk." Gracie laughs. "I mean, I joke, but not really. We both enjoy collecting and tinkering, and it made more sense to turn it into a business. Building the Emporium was perfect. We make enough to get by and support our hobbies, but we're not so busy with customers that we can't do our own thing." She tilts her head to study Jay. "Are you thinking about settling down?"

He frowns in surprise, then lets the question ride a moment. An honest question deserves a thought-through response. "Nah," he finally says. "I'm not sure what I'm thinking about."

"If you could go anywhere, where would it be?"

"The *Nanshe*," Jay says; he doesn't have to think about that — Alusina's miraculous apples be damned. "I've flown with Las for years, and somebody's got to keep her out of trouble. Plus I like the work, I like the travel. Always meeting new people."

"And leaving them behind," says Gracie.

"Part of the job."

"I think that's what I liked most about the collective. I got the thrill of travel with the supply runs, but I had a family to come home to. I would have gone stir-crazy living on a ship full time." She lifts her gaze to the ceiling again. "Your captain seems fine with it, though. Does she really always stay on the ship?"

"She does." And it's Jay's job to make sure that remains a safe option for them all. He glances around the workshop, an idea forming. "Maybe you can help us with something," he says. He's had enough talk about hopes and dreams; time to move on to the safer territory of machines and mechanics. "We need to disguise the *Nanshe*. Ruby and I had some ideas for the transponder and signature, but we could use some work on the outside and the shuttles."

"Definitely." Gracie pulls herself to her feet with an "oomph," and Jay follows her to the far corner of her workshop. "It should be easy enough to make aesthetic changes. Those Mapalad Lowboys don't have much in the way of weapons, do they?"

"No, ma'am."

"Or kitchen amenities, unless you've made some upgrades there."

"We got a new rehydrator in Artemis City a few weeks ago."

Gracie winces. "Rehydrated food will kill you faster than pirates out in the black. I modified some gear to work on my supply-run ship back when we were still working for the collective; I think I still have it lying around." She waves a hand at the workshop clutter. "As you can see, I still have most things lying around."

"That would be incredible. I wouldn't mind being able to cook again."

"You have a favorite dish?"

"My grandma's korris recipe — she moved to Corusca from New Sarjun and brought it with her. I'd love to make it for you all here, if we have the time. And if you don't mind spice."

"Bring it on." Gracie pulls a tarp off a bulky machine in the corner. "Actually I have something fun I've been playing around with, if you don't mind experimental tech."

Jay frowns at it, trying to make sense of the wires and angles. "I'm game. What does it do?"

Gracie grins. "Oh. You're gonna love it."

CHAPTER 7
LASADI

THE TRAVELER'S EMPORIUM IS QUIET BUT FOR THE SOUNDS OF the systems keeping all their fragile human bodies alive. Gentle hums from the heaters, the click and sigh of the air recyclers, quiet creaking from the metal plates that seal out the void. No one had given Lasadi directions, but it isn't hard to find her way from the dock to the store — an enormous neon pink arrow points to the lift shaft, with dancing holographic letters reading *Traveler's Emporium this way!*

She'd left Raj sleeping in her bed, dressed quietly after her shower without seeming to wake him; now she steps lightly onto the spiral staircase encircling the lift shaft. There's a button to call the lift platform, but she doesn't know what kind of ruckus that will make, and she's fairly certain she's the sole person awake in the station this early.

Or, maybe not.

She peers down the shaft as it spirals. It goes five more levels down, at least, though it's hard to tell the exact number in the dark. The next level down has another neon pink arrow on the landing, along with the word *Welcome!*

The level is dark, but someone is moving, humming softly to themselves.

Lasadi pauses on the landing. "Hello?"

"Hello there!" a voice calls back. "Turn on the lights if you need them, there's a switch at the landing."

Lasadi finds the switch, which is painted in blue and white stripes and outlined by an orange glow. When she flips it, overhead lights flicker on to reveal rows of shelves stocked with spare parts and freeze-dried meals, a cooler filled with bulbs of beer and bags of wine and liquor, pieces of environment suits, flower-print dresses and other clothing, toiletries, electronics, knick-knacks of all sorts.

And a woman with long white hair pulled into a loose braid, sitting at a counter with what looks like a nav panel dismantled in front of her, deftly twisting the wires together and capping them by touch. This has to be Vash, Lasadi recognizes her from the vid calls she's sent Raj.

"Come on in," Vash says, carefully feeling for another set of wires in the bundle. "You must be one of Raj's friends. We don't have any other guests at the moment."

"I'm Lasadi Cazinho," Lasadi says. "Captain of the *Nanshe*." Her hand flexes at her side, but she doesn't offer it. Vash's own hands are preoccupied with delicate work, and even if she wasn't busy, she wouldn't see Lasadi's gesture.

"It's good to meet you," Vash says. "Forgive me for not getting up, I'll lose my place if I stop now."

"Of course."

Lasadi pulls out a stool and sits, watching as Vash pairs the next set of wires, red to red, then cuts the housing and twists the strands together.

"Did you get in all right last night?" Vash smiles warmly in Lasadi's direction, her gaze resting somewhere between her work and Lasadi's shoulder.

"We did, thank you." Lasadi clears her throat and casts around for a conversation topic. She isn't one for small talk in the best of times — she'll leave that to the others any day. "You have quite the eclectic shop."

"Thank you! Something for everyone, and a bit more. The only thing you won't find for sale at the Emporium is weapons."

"Raj said you have decent defenses."

"We have our own ways of staying out of trouble around here."

Vash's fingers seek out another pair of wires: gold to gold. She cuts the housing and twists the strands, and Lasadi hesitates, dying to know and not sure if the question is rude. But finally, "How do you know which colors are which?" she asks.

Vash gives her a secret smile. "Every color has its own feel," she says. "Greens, blacks, reds — they *feel* different." She holds out the mass of wires. "Here. Close your eyes and choose the matching pair."

Feeling foolish, Lasadi runs her fingers over the wires, sensing nothing but rubbery plastic housing. There are six unmatched wires left, and no amount of concentration makes any of them stand out from the rest.

She finally chooses two at random and opens her eyes. "Orange and purple," she says. "I can't feel any difference. It's incredible you can."

Vash starts laughing as she takes the wires Lasadi is holding. She drops the purple, combing fingers through the rest until she finds the other orange.

"I notched the corresponding wires before I cut them out of the last nav panel," she says with a grin. She twists the wires together and caps them, then runs a thumbnail down the side. Now that Las is looking for it, she can see the faint hashmark nicks in the housing. "Sighted people are so gullible. No offense."

"That was fair play," Lasadi says, laughing. "Are we the only two up?"

"Probably. I haven't heard anyone else moving around." Vash matches the final pairs quickly, then wipes her hands down the front of her apron. "Give us a hand with breakfast, will you? Gracie normally isn't up for hours, and she won't be coherent until after she's had her coffee."

Lasadi stands when Vash does; the older woman flicks out a thin telescoping cane and uses it to navigate the shelving units to the lift shaft, down the spiral staircase to what must be their living quarters. It's an eclectically decorated open space. A lounge area off the landing is filled with colorful textiles, throw rugs, and a pair of mismatched couches and armchairs set up for entertaining. The kitchen and dining area are on the other side of the staircase, featuring a massive table that could easily seat ten. Four doors set at even intervals lead deeper into the level — likely to bedrooms and bathrooms. Art hangs from every wall, and every surface is covered with objects, many of which look antique.

"You must enjoy entertaining," Lasadi says. "This space is incredible."

Vash's smile lights up her face. "We don't get many visitors, but most of those who come through are quite special." She crosses to the kitchen, slipping the telescoping cane into a pocket once her palm hits the countertop. "It's nice to feed someone who cares what the food tastes like, too. Gracie's a fine cook, but she gets so lost in projects. She'll pop something in the oven and then get an idea and run out to her workshop. I'll only know it happened once I smell the burning. Start the coffee? The machine's by the stove."

Lasadi finds coffee grounds in a canister beside the machine and measures out a good amount. The rich scent of coffee soon fills the kitchen.

Vash takes a deep, happy breath through her nose.

"That'll bring them running." While Lasadi was working, Vash had pulled out vegetables and a cutting board, and is now cutting tomatoes into precise rounds. Lasadi's mouth waters at the anticipation of fresh produce. "Pour me a cup? Black."

Lasadi does, sets it with an audible *clink* on the counter in front of her; Vash brushes her fingers against it, then goes back to slicing tomatoes.

"How long have you known Raj?" Lasadi hopes it sounds like a normal question a captain would ask of a crewmate, but the corner of Vash's mouth curls in a knowing smile. Olds, what has Raj told them about her?

"A handful of years," Vash says. "We used to have a couple of freelancers who would procure the more interesting things we need, but Raj always goes above and beyond." She smiles. "He's been under a shadow, though — more and more every time we talked. It's been nice to hear him laugh again."

Lasadi clears her throat. "There's been a lot more laughter on the *Nanshe* since he came aboard."

"That's good," Vash says. "Laughter is as precious a commodity out here as air and fuel."

"And tomatoes."

Vash smiles and plucks a slice off her growing pile, offering it to Lasadi. It's sweet and tart and *incredible*; Lasadi closes her eyes as she savors the taste.

"We grow our own," Vash says. "One of my little projects. I've been working on a prototype for smaller ships that might be ready for testing, if you're interested."

"I'd like that."

"Is that coffee?" asks a new voice, and Lasadi turns to see Gracie standing in one of the doorways wearing loose biosilk pajama pants and a magenta paisley robe; Lasadi catches a glimpse of a disheveled bedroom through the door behind her. Gracie yawns, then runs a hand through the dark, silver-swathed hair that hangs in loose waves almost down to her waist.

"You know damn well it's coffee," says Vash, setting down her knife and turning to face the newcomer. "Gracie, have you met our Captain Lasadi yet?"

"We met last night while you were getting your beauty rest."

Vash pats her own cheek with a coquettish smile. "Did it work?"

"You look like Tiyana Chary." Gracie leans to kiss her wife, then pours herself a cup of coffee and curls up on a dining chair to breathe in steam with delight.

"I only have your word that's a good thing."

"It's a good thing," agrees Lasadi. "Tiyana Chary's still making vids, and whatever cryogenic chamber they've been keeping her in these last few decades is working wonders."

"You'll make me a cryogenic chamber when I start to get too wrinkly, love?" Vash asks.

"Never," says Gracie. "I love your wrinkles."

Lasadi sips her own coffee, marveling at how comfortable the two women are with each other. The teasing, the intimate gestures with that air of companionable history. She used to have that — not in a romantic way, but in a friendly way, with her comrades at the CLA, before she took up with Anton and he systematically carved her away from them.

She has many regrets about falling for Anton Kato, but letting him pull her away from her comrades is the biggest one of all.

She's been letting him pull her away from this new crew, too, she knows. Anton may be gone — executed or imprisoned by the New Manila Liberation Front, she doesn't know which or care. She only knows she still has work to do to dismantle the emotional and physical defenses she built as a result of his control, his betrayals. She hadn't handled last night well, not at first. But once she finally allowed herself to relax — once she finally let herself trust Raj — she'd found herself in heaven. She hasn't slept that well in years, despite the unfamiliar presence in her bed.

She's kept herself under lock and key for so long. Escaping that cage for one night had been pure bliss. Could she learn to leave it behind for good?

The sound of boots in the stairwell jolts her out of her thoughts. It's coming from the dock area above, rather than the crew quarters below, and Lasadi's body grows suddenly warm, heat blooming below her sternum.

Olds, she's in deep.

"Vashti!" Raj calls from the stairwell. His grin is pure delight; Gracie waves a bleary hello and Vash sets her knife down carefully, turning to hold out her arms for Raj's hug. He squeezes tight before finally letting her go. "I see you met Lasadi." The smile he turns on Lasadi is mischievous. "Morning, Captain."

"Morning." She thinks her voice stays neutral.

"Let me get you some coffee," Vash says, but Raj squeezes her shoulder as he walks by.

"I've got it. Unless your coffee maker is some ridiculous new contraption that's going to explode on me if I try to pour a cup without my fingerprints in the system."

"Same coffee maker as always," says Vash. "Although speaking of new contraptions, I offered your captain the greenhouse prototype I've been working on."

"Does *that* explode?" Raj asks.

"Not everything I make explodes," Vash says defensively.

"The shield you gave me did."

"It was meant to." Vash turns to him, curious. "So you did test it? You never told me."

"I did," Raj says. "It's terrifying, it stings like hell, and it makes your mouth taste like burnt popcorn for a few days. But it provided the right amount of distraction to get me out of trouble when a bunch of Kasey Aherne's goons had me in their sights."

"Do you want another one? I've been working to reduce the sting."

"I'm a maybe."

"You just said it saved your life, didn't it?"

"*This* version did. But after that ring communicator you had me test, I'm spooked to try your 'new and improved' versions."

"The ring communicator?" Lasadi asks, and the story begins, Vash and Gracie telling bits of it in turns while Raj refills coffees and the others begin to trickle in, drawn by the aromas of breakfast.

Vash calls Lasadi to the kitchen to help her plate up the breakfast — an incredible-looking salad of fresh vegetables along with some sort of baked bread-and-egg casserole that smells spicy and sweet and flavorful, the crust bubbly and brown and perfect. Jay, Ruby, and Alex all seem well rested as they gather around the table, accepting mugs of coffee from Raj.

This place is magic, thinks Lasadi. The first place that's felt like home since she left her grandmother's.

Could they do this, too? Find a home base, a place to return to, a place Jay could fill with electronics, a place Ruby could have all the equipment she wants without complaining about space, a place Alex could turn into a jungle gym for practicing break-in scenarios. Somewhere she and Raj could just *be*?

You're getting ahead of yourself, Cazinho, Lasadi thinks. *One step at a time.*

Lasadi sits with her own plate, studying the faces of her little crew, letting herself enjoy the contentment she sees there before she turns to Vash and Gracie.

"Thank you for your hospitality," she says. "I hope we can repay it. Raj says you have a job for us?"

CHAPTER 8
RAJ

"A job?" Alex asks before either Vash or Gracie can speak. "Is it more alien artifacts?"

Gracie's eyebrows shoot up, but Vash's face splits in a laugh. "And what gave you the idea of aliens, young man," she says.

"I saw the pieces Raj found for you. They're alien artifacts, right?"

"There's no such thing as aliens," Ruby chides her little brother, but Vash aims a smile her way.

"That's what Gracie says, too." Vash spears another slice of tomato and chews thoughtfully. "Speaking of, you *did* bring those with you, Raj?"

"You think I'd cheat my favorite clients?" Raj had brought the pieces down with him, but hadn't wanted to shift the relaxed mood of the morning by talking business. Now Vash scoots her plate to the side and Raj removes the pieces from their wrappings, laying them on a cloth in front of her. The larger piece is an obsidian-like scepter the length of his forearm, carved with the motif of a strange, stylized bird with wings spiraling upwards. The smaller piece is carved with the same strange winged creature, and is the length of Raj's hand.

"The totem you asked for is on your left; the second piece, on your right, we found in the Liluri Mountains. And I'd be remiss not to mention Lasadi's the one who actually stole the totem from Sumilang."

"I was just faster," Lasadi says with a wry smile. "You would have gotten it eventually."

He laughs. "Maybe."

It feels like ages ago that he was standing in Parr Sumilang's museum, sparring with Lasadi for this prize. Little did he know he'd be walking away from the chance encounter with far more than a totem for Vash and Gracie.

The memory of that day rushes back: Lasadi's body pressed against his, her sly smile while she held a knife to his throat, the way she came back for him when he thought his game was up. He's seen the range of this woman since, from playful to fierce, from confident to vulnerable. He can't wait to explore the rest of her. Assuming she'll continue to have him.

He's still watching her; he shoves the thoughts aside and forces himself back to the now before things get awkward. Across the table, Vash's fingertips carefully trace the lines of the original totem before she begins to explore the second one.

"What are they?" Alex asks.

"Artifacts from an old cult," says Gracie. "The Tisare, who believed atmosphere was unclean. According to their teachings, humans originally left Earth in ancient times in order to ascend to a higher plane of existence where they didn't rely on a planet. They believed our ancestors sinned by colonizing Indira and New Sarjun rather than staying on the *Ark Matsya* and fulfilling our final form."

"They were some of the earliest settlers in Durga's Belt," Vash adds. "The cult's extinct now, but you still find their artifacts around." She carefully lifts the second object and hands it to Gracie. "You found this one on Indira?"

"A cave in the Liluri Mountains in New Manila," confirms Raj. "We were searching for some experimental Alliance aircraft that was rumored to have crashed there."

"Experimental *alien* aircraft," corrects Alex. "I saw that thing in the water. You can't convince me humans made it."

"A cave?" Gracie asks, and Raj begins to describe the crash site: the carved statues surrounding the pool in the center of the cave, the hidden cache. Alex jumps in to continue the story with fantastical descriptions of the ambush that had interrupted their search, and how his fast-thinking and explosive plan saved them all. Alex doesn't bring up Anton, or the NMLF, not that it would matter here. But the kid is good at telling an engaging story with the incriminating information filed off, Raj notes with satisfaction.

Alex also doesn't tell the part where Lasadi fooled them all into thinking she suspected Raj of betraying them, when it had been Anton all along. By the shadow on Lasadi's face, though, the guilt still stings. He catches her eye, a smile to let her know he doesn't harbor any resentment. On the contrary. What she did took an iron spine, and was admirable as hell.

Once he realized it was a ruse, at least.

Ruby kicks him under the table and Raj jumps, turns back to Vash, heat rising under his collar. He's been staring again. Maybe someday it'll be possible to be in the same room as Lasadi without his attention being completely absorbed by her presence, but not right now, not after last night.

"So, it's aliens, right?" Alex asks when he's done regaling Vash and Gracie with tales of their escape.

"That's one of the theories," says Vash, and smiles. "Gracie's rolling her eyes, isn't she?"

"Never, my love."

"Her and Ruby both," says Alex. "My sister doesn't believe in aliens."

"Course I believe in aliens, don't I," says Ruby. "It's mathematics, only. But here? In our system? We'd know."

"Maybe the Tisare knew," Vash says, then holds up a hand. "And we can argue about all that later, I can hear you getting ready to, Graciela." She takes a deep breath, expression becoming serious, and the energy around the room shifts. Gracie squeezes her wife's hand, then silently rises to collect empty plates while Vash begins to talk.

"A friend of ours recently passed away," she says.

"I'm sorry," Raj says; grief creases the corners of Vash's eyes.

"Heart attack," Gracie says from the kitchen counter. "I kept telling him he needed to take better care of himself. Age isn't always kind, out here."

"He was an inventor," Vash says. "He would stop in for parts and to trade stories whenever he was in the area. When we first met he had a storefront in Ironfall, but in the past few years he'd gotten a yen to wander. He rented a stall on the *Slingshot*, and that's where he was when he passed. His cargo is still on board."

"You can live on the *Slingshot*?" Alex asks, his eyes wide and curious.

"Some people do," Vash says. "Merchants and such."

"Sounds fun," Alex says.

Ruby shoots him a skeptical look. "Does it, though."

Raj has never seen the *Slingshot*, that vast, strange ship that ferries passengers from the Pearls out into the deeper reaches of Durga's Belt. It's part passenger transport, part cargo modules, part roving space station where other small ships can dock and get a tow. It might be slower than traveling under your own power, but catching that tow is efficient if you're traveling a ways. It's nice not to worry about running out of fuel or supplies a week from the nearest station.

The area of the Belt within a few days' flight of the Pearls is the most heavily populated part, though there are a few major stations like Maribi and Tal Vera that support a healthy population. Of course, the flip side is that the asteroids closest to the Pearls have been picked over for everything but the most common minerals. If you want to strike it rich, you need to be willing to go farther out.

That's where the *Slingshot* comes in. It's technically a public service administered by the Pearls Federation. In reality, though, it's far enough removed from the Federation's oversight to be its own unique beast.

"What happens to your belongings if you die on the *Slingshot*?" Lasadi asks.

"It's a legal gray area," Vash says. "Karl had no next of kin, and he didn't officially file any after-death instructions for his property. He always told us he'd leave a note to deliver his wreckage back to the Emporium, but if he did, no one is willing to honor it."

"Because the director of the *Slingshot* took everything," says Gracie bitterly.

"Hush. You don't know that's true."

Raj glances between the two women. "What do you mean?"

"We don't know anything for sure," Vash says before Gracie can answer. "But Karl had mentioned he was planning on going into business with the director. He had some invention they were going to partner on selling together."

"But something spooked him," Gracie cuts in. "The last message he sent said he was backing out of the deal."

"Do you know if he did?" Raj asks.

Gracie shakes her head. "We're not sure if he had a chance."

"It was all the stress," Vash says. "Karl never handled stress well."

"He didn't," Gracie says, laying a hand on her wife's shoulder. The look she cuts Raj says she doesn't quite believe it was simple stress that caused their friend's heart attack. "It's not Karl's cargo we're so concerned about, anyway. Karl's mind was brilliant, and he tinkered with dangerous ideas. His belongings won't be particularly valuable to a government official, but his notes shouldn't fall into the wrong hands."

"Exactly," says Vash. "If the Federation gets them — or one of the cartels?"

Lasadi leans forward. "What did your friend sell on the *Slingshot*?"

"He was experimenting with a new sort of AI," says Vash. "A companion. It was supposed to be an aid for old wanderers like himself, or for miners. He thought if he could figure out how to manufacture it cheaply enough, it would make life better for those who keep heading out into the black. His invention was supposed to be adaptable enough to help you with anything you needed. External repairs of a ship, mining, all of that. He planned to sell the basic unit along with modular kits and plans people could build themselves." She smiles sadly. "He always said no one is more inventive than those who make their living in the black."

Ruby had pulled out her tablet the minute Vash started talking. "This guy?" she asks, turning the tablet around to display a photo. "Oh, sorry," she says quickly at Vash's frown. "Karl Gatmaitan, kind of an older guy with amazing eyebrows."

Vash laughs. "That's him."

"There are a few inventor boards he's pretty active on," Ruby says. "He's not too subtle about the ideas he's been working on."

Which is another thing that could have made Karl a target. There are plenty of ways to make a murder seem like a heart attack — and even more ways when no one's around to see the body for themselves. Raj shares a glance with Ruby; she's clearly thinking the same thing.

"We can help," Lasadi says. "We'd be happy to."

"Just return his notes to us," Gracie says. "We'd like to continue his project, but we need his plans — and to make sure anything else he might have been working on doesn't get to the wrong people."

"Where's the *Slingshot* now?" Lasadi asks Ruby.

"It made its pass by the Pearls and it's heading out again," Ruby answers. "We can catch it, but we'll need to be fast. We hold off too much longer, we'll burn too much fuel getting there."

"Then let's get moving sooner rather than later," Lasadi says. "Jay?"

"Gracie and I talked last night about the modifications we want to make to the *Nanshe*," Jay says. "We should be able to finish the work by tonight."

Gracie nods. "I'll go pull aside some things."

"Show them the greenhouse prototype," Vash says. "And anything else you think would be fun."

"I'll supervise," Raj says. "I know what your idea of 'fun' is, Vashti."

"Spoilsport." Vash smiles. "Ruby?"

"Yes?"

Vash's face turns towards Ruby's voice. "Do you have a minute? Raj mentioned you wanted information on your parents, and I'd like to hear more. Gracie and I are old as the heavens and have met plenty of people in our day. Maybe there's a way we can help."

Ruby shoots him a quizzical look as she settles back at the table; she's too curious to be upset with him for sharing her business with strangers.

Alex hovers at her shoulder. "Should I stay?"

"Help the others, will you?" Ruby says; she tosses a smile his way and turns back to Vash too quick to catch the flash of pain on her brother's face. "I'll fill you in when we're moving."

"C'mon." Raj elbows Alex. "Let's go see what goodies Gracie's got in her workshop."

He squeezes Vash's shoulder as he walks by, hiding his own pang of disappointment. He'd hoped to spend a few more days with Vash and Gracie — and it would be incredible to have the *Nanshe* to themselves for another few nights. But the timeline is the timeline, and it's probably safest for Vash and Gracie if the *Nanshe* keeps moving, with Raj on it.

CHAPTER 9
JAY

THE AROMA IS MAGICAL: BUTTER AND SUGAR AND CINNAMON drifting through the normally sterile air of the *Nanshe*. The ship's air scrubbers do their best to erase all trace of the five humans living in close quarters aboard, and eventually they'll scrub this glorious scent away, too. But for now Jay leans in to the new oven unit, eyes closed, filling his lungs with joy.

"Are you making *cookies*?"

Raj's voice behind him is incredulous, and Jay smiles. Lets himself float back gently to face Raj.

"Cinnamon rolls," Jay corrects. "The *Nanshe*'s kitchen got an upgrade, since we were doing the work anyway. Your friends are goddesses. Genius goddesses."

"What would your old ones say to hear you talking blasphemy?"

Jay glances at the ceiling, towards the bridge where Lasadi keeps the little Coruscan mixla statue she stole from Sumilang along with the Tisare totem. He'd already planned to drop a square of cinnamon roll in the stasis field as a thank-you.

"If they have a sense of smell, they're thinking the same

thing." Jay glances at the timer. The unit will turn off automatically when it's done cooking, which Vash had teased Gracie about including so that she wouldn't get distracted and burn something down. Lasadi's ensconced on the bridge, and Ruby and Alex are both in their rooms. The smell of cinnamon rolls will bring everyone to the kitchen soon enough, but they've got some time.

Jay jerks his chin at the ladder down to the cargo bay level. "I need to check on something in the engine room," he says. "You got a minute?"

Raj follows him down. The ladder deposits them between a pair of doors — to Jay's quarters and the spare crew cabin. The engine room is behind them, along with more storage and the open cargo bay. The cargo level's gotten a lot more crowded than when it was just him and Las on the *Nanshe*. A few more pieces of equipment in the workout area, more supplies in the storage closet. At least they're not having to work around that mining skiff they'd recovered from the scrappers anymore. They left that behind with Vash and Gracie for the Ahmadi family to pick up.

"What's on your mind?" Raj asks when Jay settles on a crate well out of earshot from anyone up the ladder in the galley.

Jay takes a deep breath; he's been fishing for a delicate way to ask this and coming up blank. Best to say it. "I know it's none of my business, but. You've seen what happened to her?" And at Raj's quizzical look: "The scars."

Raj clears his throat. "Are you trying to ask if we're sleeping together?"

"Nah, man. Everybody knows you're finally sleeping together." Jay's smile doesn't linger. "I'm trying to ask how she is. Since the accident she's kept herself covered chin to toe, and she shuts me down when I've tried to bring it up."

He doesn't blame her for it; they both lost so much that

day. Jay's dealt with his own shit — finding someone to talk to was one of the first things he did once he knew Las would live and they'd be staying in Ironfall for a while. He didn't think twice about it. He's known too many veterans in his life to assume he could deal with the nightmares without professional help.

Lasadi, though? He'd tried to save her life three years ago, but he'd only resurrected a ghost. She's kept him close since, but at arm's length. And at that impossible distance, he'd watched the friend he loved and followed slowly fade.

Until Raj arrived.

Keeping Lasadi in the air had been his purpose while they flew together for the CLA, and keeping her afloat had been his obsession for the past three years. Doing so had consumed him, burned him nearly into a shell of himself, and he doesn't think he'd still be here on the *Nanshe* if Raj hadn't crashed into their lives.

Scratch that. He absolutely wouldn't be here.

"I know how bad it *was*," Jay says. "I was there — in the crash, while she was in the regen tanks. But I don't know how bad it *is*. She needs to talk about what happened. It doesn't have to be with me, but she needs to talk." Jay sighs. "Like I said. It's probably none of my business."

"You know Lasadi," Raj says. "She'd say it's none of my business either."

"Yeah." It's why they're having this conversation in the cargo bay while Las is busy on the bridge. Jay knows exactly how pissed she'd be if she knew they were talking about her — let alone talking about her scars. But it's not just curiosity fueling Jay's question. This is important.

And by the conflict on Raj's face, the other man can tell it's important, too. Curiosity and worry war with Raj's obvious desire to respect Las's privacy, until:

"You were with her, right?" Raj asks. "You got shot

down together at the Battle of Tannis. Unless you don't want to talk about it, either."

It's a smart question; it keeps them both off the tricky ground of talking directly about Las.

"Happy to." It's not a story Jay loves remembering, but it's his. And years of dealing with it instead of repressing it have turned it into a story he can use, rather than one that uses him. "We got hit coming out of our final run — a run that a lot of Mercury Squadron didn't come back from. None of us really expected to, it was a last-ditch effort to slow down the Alliance while Tannis was evacuated."

A muscle jumps in Raj's jaw, but he doesn't speak. While Las and Jay and the rest of Mercury Squadron fought desperately to save any civilians they could, Raj had been on the other side. Knowing the orders to bomb Tannis were coming but powerless to stop the massacre while in Alliance custody.

"Our fighter was losing power fast. I knew how bad a shape our ship was in — I was trying to hold us together. But I didn't know how bad a shape Las was in. She told me she was fine and got us the hell out of danger." He scrubs a hand over the back of his neck. "Well, almost. She passed out while we were mid-rendezvous with some of Nico Garnet's mercs. Their crew got us the rest of the way."

When he takes a breath to continue, he can almost taste the memory of charred metal and scorched flesh; the faint thread of butter and cinnamon in the air seems a lifetime away.

"I thought she was dead, once I got myself out and got to her. The cockpit was almost destroyed — the systems had put the fire out, but she'd taken a bolt of shrapnel to the side, through the hull. We had to cut her out."

"Gods."

"They weren't going to." This is the part Jay hates to

tell, but what he did next is as much a part of his story as the rest. "Didn't want to waste resources on a lost cause."

Raj's breath comes sharp. "What did you do?"

"I pulled a gun on the ship's medic." Jay's lips quirk into a rueful smile. "Said I'd take as many as the bastards down as I could unless they agreed to treat her. I didn't care what they did to me — I heard a lot of my friends die over the comms that day, and I didn't want to live if I lost her, too."

"So they helped her at gunpoint."

"I had to put the gun away eventually and pick up some forceps. They weren't lying about the lack of resources. I learned quick how to be a surgeon's assistant for a day."

The ship's medic had agreed to operate, but since they couldn't spare any other medical personnel, it had been Jay at the medic's side. Jay knows how to be a helper from his years of working with his father, and he'd handed the medic unfamiliar tools when called for, held clamps and gauze when instructed. Once he'd shut down his panic, the role had felt vaguely familiar. Only instead of being stained to the elbow by engine grease at the end, he'd been covered in Lasadi's blood.

In his nightmares, he's always trapped and helpless, unable to do anything but listen as the voices of people he loves are cut off one by one. They've lessened through the years, but they haven't gone away entirely. And new voices have joined the chorus. Raj, Ruby, Alex, Chiara — they've all had cameos in his nightmares.

Never Las, though. Maybe it's because he was able to do something to help her in the end.

Raj is watching him, quiet. "The burn scars are pretty extensive," he finally says. "I'm sure you've guessed. From knee to shoulder and all down her back. And she's got a nasty scar in her side, must be from the shrapnel."

"Is she still in pain?" It's what Jay really needs to know. "She says she's not, but she's good at hiding it."

Raj shakes his head and Jay's eyes close in relief. Thank the old ones.

"I have no fucking idea how she managed to fly us out," Jay says after a moment. "That woman scares me."

Raj laughs. "Same." He tilts his head, studying Jay a moment. "How are *you* doing with all of this?"

"I wasn't injured. Not a scratch."

"Not physically."

"Course." Jay shrugs. "Like I said, I've got someone to talk to. A professional — been seeing a therapist since I was a kid. I know the value of getting things off your chest."

Raj's eyebrows draw together. "Because of your transition?"

Something light and golden bubbles up through the heaviness of the conversation; Jay can't help but laugh. "That's not how I meant it, but good one."

Raj looks confused a moment, then winces as he realizes why Jay's laughing. "'Getting things off your chest,'" he says, and soon he's laughing, too. "Sorry."

"I go because it's healthy." Jay smiles at him. "I keep telling Las, but she never listens. Maybe she'll listen to you."

Raj shakes his head. "I doubt it."

"Maybe she'll talk to you, then."

"I hope so."

Jay takes Raj's outstretched hand and the other man pulls him into a hug. "I think those cinnamon rolls are ready," Jay says; he can hear the others' voices from the kitchen. "We better go get some before they're gone."

CHAPTER 10
LASADI

IN THE THREE DAYS SINCE THEY LEFT THE TRAVELER'S Emporium, Lasadi has eaten incredibly well.

Pasta, salads, curries, and Jay had finally made his grandmother's korris, which was shockingly good even if it had pushed the *Nanshe*'s recyclers to their limits trying to clear eye-watering capsaicin from the air when Jay fried the dried peppers. It turns out he and Raj are both adept cooks when given the right equipment, and Lasadi's taste buds have been delighting in the shift from rehydrated meals.

Or maybe Lasadi is finally letting herself savor food again.

Because the food isn't the only thing that's improved on the *Nanshe* these past few days. She'd been terrified that dropping her professional boundaries with Raj would damage the crew dynamic, but it's done the opposite. No one has reacted poorly to their relationship being out in the open; in fact, the remaining tension has drained from the small group. In retrospect, she and Raj hadn't exactly been hiding their feelings.

It feels so good. Too good. *Precarious*, a voice whispers in the back of her mind. One false move and it could all come crashing down, voices silenced one by one in the black. Las takes a sharp breath, banishing the thought. Letting that notion haunt her is a surefire way to turn it into a self-fulfilling prophecy.

Lasadi cracks her neck and closes the hologram plans of the *Slingshot* she's been studying. The others will be gathering soon in the galley below to finalize their plan; they'll rendezvous with the *Slingshot* soon.

She checks her messages. She missed a call from Tora Garnet, who left no message. Probably means Tora has a job for them, but she promised Jay no more Garnet jobs, so she ignores it. As she starts to stand, though, her comm chimes with another incoming message. A glance at the sender washes ice through her gut: Evvi Faye Cazinho.

Olds be damned.

Lasadi swipes the vid open, finger hesitating over Play. She's been checking her messages with increasing dread for days, trying to work out what it meant that it's taken her sister so long to respond to the note Lasadi sent from Sapis. The delay means either her sister gave herself time to cool down first, or that she's worked herself up to a finer fury.

In the paused vid, Evvi Faye is perfectly made-up. Lasadi studies the stylish coif, the cutting angle of her eyeliner, the power-red lip. Makeup has always been one of Evvi's most effective pieces of armor, and Lasadi guesses her sister's at her most battle-ready. It makes her look fierce — and gorgeous. She'd always had their mother's darker hair, a curly chestnut to Lasadi's wavy dirty blond, their mother's full lips, that same dark sparkle in her eyes. But in the past three years she's somehow transformed from an awkward university student to a confident young woman.

Ruby's laugh sounds from the galley as the crew begins to gather. Lasadi's finger still hovers over Play. She should probably wait to watch this vid — she needs to be in the right headspace to finalize these plans, and whatever Evvi has to say will be hard to hear. But. She'll be distracted and dying of curiosity if she waits until after the crew meeting.

She steels herself and hits Play.

"I'm sorry, but are you fucking serious?" Evvi Faye's opening line confirms that her delay in replying wasn't because she was busy. She was taking the time to properly whip herself into a fury. Lasadi winces and settles against her chair to listen.

"I didn't even know how to answer your last message," Evvi continues. "I was too mad at you to even reply. Can you tell? I'm just so fucking — olds, I can't even describe how much I hate you right now."

"Sorry, Evvi," Lasadi murmurs into the pause while her sister collects herself.

"It's been *three years*, Lala. I have been putting offerings in the family altar for *three years* do you even know what that was like for me? For all of us? You know Amit and Bella have a baby now, and one of the first things I did was take him to the altar and show him your picture and say, 'Hey, you've got an aunt, but she died before you were born.' You have a fucking one-year-old *nephew*? And you've been *hiding*? And letting us think you're *dead*? What the hell is wrong with you."

Evvi Faye takes a deep, ragged breath.

"You know, don't bother telling me what your reason was. You're going to say something like it kept us safe, or you're wanted by the Alliance, or whatever, but it's total bullshit. I'm your sister. You let me think you were dead because you didn't trust me to protect you, and that's the worst feeling in the world. Lala, I'm so happy you're alive, and I'm so absolutely fucking furious I can't see straight. I hope you're delighted with yourself."

Evvi scrapes an angry fingernail across her eyelashes to collect a stray tear, then reaches forward as though to cut off the recording before straightening once more in afterthought.

"Oh. By the way, I haven't told Amit or Grandma, you have to do that yourself and I'm not going to make your job any easier. But you better do it soon because they think I'm crying all the time these days because of a breakup. Which, asshole, I'm also going through. Great fucking timing for coming back to life." Evvi sighs and shakes her head, then reaches to end the recording again. "I love you, I hate you," she says. "I'm going to go right now and take your picture off the altar, so you better call Grandma soon or I'll tell her I found out you defected to the Alliance or started a sex cult or something equally awful. I'm serious."

The recording ends, looping back to the opening image of Evvi Faye's furiously made-up face from before she started crying and her eye makeup smeared.

Lasadi takes a deep breath, lets it out slow. She definitely should have waited to watch that vid.

"Las?" She blinks at Jay's voice below her, and a moment later he's up the ladder and floating into the co-pilot's chair. "Everyone's in the kitchen, we're ready for you." And he tilts his head, noticing what she's been watching. "Who's that?"

"My sister," Lasadi says. Jay's still studying the paused vid, a curious expression on his face.

"She looks different than you," he says finally. "I thought your family didn't know you were alive."

"Well, Evvi Faye knows now, and she's pissed."

"Of course she is." Jay gives Evvi's hologram another long look, then squeezes Lasadi's shoulder. "C'mon. I'll help you brainstorm how to make it up to her later."

Lasadi returns his smile, but she's not quite sure how that's possible.

"You let me think you were dead because you didn't trust me to protect you," Evvi had said, and the worst part is she's right. Mostly. Anton had primed Lasadi not to trust anyone but him, and he'd said her family had held banishing after she was reported dead, named her as a war criminal with no place on the family altar. She shouldn't have believed him, but he'd eroded her own faith in herself so badly she'd accepted his cold, bitter version of her family as fact.

She'd let her family think she was dead not because she didn't trust them, but because she didn't trust herself.

Olds. How can she ever explain *that*? How can she tell Evvi she fell for Anton's grift and let him destroy her, that she's not the strong, confident older sister Evvi always believed her to be?

Somehow, she'll figure it out. And she won't have to do it alone, because as she follows Jay into the galley, the rest of her small crew turns to face her, and she knows that whatever the problem — from stolen skiffs to devastated sisters — they've got her back.

If only she could figure out why.

Everyone is at their usual place around the galley table, already studying a holographic image of the *Slingshot* in the center. Alex is at the far end, conveniently located next to the rack of hot sauces. Ruby's at his right with a space beside her for Jay, Raj at his left.

By the time Lasadi takes her place closest to the bridge, she's feeling calm again.

"All right," she says. "What have we got?"

"A giant space train," says Alex. "I can't wait to rob it."

"We might need a more sophisticated plan than 'Alex robs the space train,'" says Lasadi. "The *Slingshot*'s both complicated and well defended, which means we need to be inside to get anywhere. Ruby, did you find out what happened to Vash and Gracie's friend?"

"I found the official version: heart attack, end of story.

Body's been cremated and sent to the stars already, so there's no way to verify the doctor's report."

"Do you believe the report?"

"I never believe anything I didn't see with my own eyes."

Ruby rotates the hologram in the center of the table to show full length of the *Slingshot*. Its chain of connected modules looks an awful lot like the maglev trains that haul cargo planetside. Ruby highlights three cylindrical modules near the front.

"Passage on the *Slingshot* comes in a few different flavors," Ruby says. "Module A is the director's living quarters, the modules chaining after that are for staff and passengers. Each comes with its own services — hygiene units, basic food available at autocafes and vending machines. They also each have their own external control units in case there's a disaster, or so they can reconfigure if they need to ship more cargo, or have more living units, or whatever."

"Is there a first class?" asks Raj.

"So you don't have to brush shoulders with the rest of us, love?" Ruby winks at him, then highlights Module C. "There is, but barely. Difference is you get your own bathroom and access to the first-class lounge — but it's never fully booked. Doesn't seem to be a market for anything terribly plush."

"Anyone who can afford a first-class ticket can probably afford their own transportation," guesses Lasadi.

"Exactly. And speaking of . . ." Ruby swipes along the length of the *Slingshot*, past the rest of the cylindrical passenger modules, past an egg-shaped module, to the *Slingshot*'s tail. The tail is comprised of a half-dozen long, narrow modules with airlocks built in a spiral pattern.

"Here's what our ticket gets us," Ruby says. "A berth for the *Nanshe* on Module E, the first docking module. It's basically a central corridor with a services hub on one end, like the ones in the passenger modules. Showers, community kitchen, a couple bars."

"And this bit in the middle?" Lasadi asks, pointing to the enormous egg-shaped section between the passenger modules and Module E.

"This is where our friend Karl Gatmaitan spent the final year of his life," Ruby says, and nods to Raj.

"Very dramatic handoff, thank you for that," Raj says. "This is the marketplace module. It's lined with vendor stalls, some of which are owned by the management, though most are rented out to people like Karl Gatmaitan. Gatmaitan sold odds and ends to everyone who passed through the *Slingshot*, making enough of a living to get by without being wildly successful. And about a month ago, he was found dead in his bunk."

"So the administration confiscated his belongings?" Lasadi asks.

"There's a clause in the vendor agreement," Ruby says. "And a sneaky one in the docking agreement, too."

Lasadi frowns. "What do you mean?"

"It's not sinister. But if a ship is abandoned on the *Slingshot*, the next of kin have two weeks to recover it before it becomes property of the agency."

"That's not much time. Especially out here."

"Still. It makes sense. They can't afford to haul owner-less ships around the black, and a ship like this can't just turn around and deliver a ship back to Artemis."

"How often does that happen?" Lasadi asks.

"I'll find out."

"So the clause in the vendor agreement overrules Karl Gatmaitan's wishes to have his belongings transferred to Vash and Gracie."

"It does," Ruby confirms. "And instead it transfers them to this guy here."

A man's face replaces the holographic plans of the *Slingshot*.

"Daniel Escat. For fifteen years, he's been director of the company that administers the *Slingshot*. This isn't the first complaint against him for confiscating cargo."

"Wait," Alex says. "If there have been complaints against him, why hasn't the Federation done anything?"

"The *Slingshot* is basically its own company," Ruby says. "Federation can't do much."

"But it's a public service, right?" Alex asks. "Don't they appoint the job?"

Ruby shrugs. "They do, but no one else wants it. Living on a giant space train isn't most people's cup of tea, and the Federation has bigger problems closer to home. Unless this Daniel Escat guy starts murdering people, they'll leave him alone."

"How do we know he's not murdering people?" Raj asks.

Lasadi frowns at him. "You think Gatmaitan was murdered?"

"Gracie said he sounded worried in the last message he sent. The director could have staged an accident to keep him from backing out of their deal."

"Or someone got wind of what he was working on," Ruby says.

"Maybe," Lasadi allows. "But we have no evidence."

"Worth looking into, though," Jay says mildly; Lasadi holds up her hands.

"Keep your ears open. But as of now the plan is to get Karl Gatmaitan's notes, get out, get back to Vash and Gracie. This is supposed to be a simple job. We don't need to go complicating it with theories."

"We'll need to get through Escat to get the notes," Ruby says. "All Karl's belongings have been transferred to a secure vault in the director's module."

"Easy, then," Alex says. "A quick spacewalk, override the maintenance access, grab the loot, slip back out. Like that salvage op."

"We might need to be subtler than the salvage op," Lasadi says.

"I can be subtle."

"Let's try talking our way in first," Lasadi says. "Ruby, what does Escat want?"

"Well." Ruby leans forward and swipes away the hologram of his bust to go back to the schematic of the *Slingshot*. "He's a man who enjoys his luxuries, and he's built up quite the little empire of mining claims. Our Mr. Escat fancies himself as something of an investor. He likes to say he's lucky, but I imagine it doesn't hurt that everyone on the *Slingshot* is on their way to or from a secret mining claim — there are rumors Escat expects a cut from anyone who's had a windfall and wants a ride back."

"Extortion?"

"The *Slingshot* is the only ride a lot of these folks have," Ruby says. "He can charge what he wants."

"So Escat's got a taste for luxury," Raj says. "We can work with that."

"Grab his attention with a mining claim?" Lasadi asks.

"We sweeten the deal," Raj says. "Not just a claim, but a new way of making his current claims even more profitable."

Jay straightens. "Namidium."

"Exactly."

"What's that?" Lasadi asks.

"The most valuable mineral in the system at the moment," Jay says. "Used to manufacture next-gen propulsion drives — like the new booster we had installed on the *Nanshe* a few months back. But it's almost impossible to test for unless you ship your samples back to a lab in the Pearls. People have been working on ways to find namidium more reliably on-site, but no one's come up with one."

"Got it," Lasadi says. "So Escat probably already has namidium in his claims, but no way to easily detect it. If we can interest him, we're in. Is that something you and Ruby can do?"

"Why not?" Ruby says. "Jay and I will solve the unsolvable problem, won't we. And in" — she glances at the time readout — "fifteen hours, only."

"It just needs to be good enough to get us access to the director's module," Lasadi says. "I'm sure Raj can work his magic with whatever you give him." She shares a smile with him, giving herself permission to enjoy the warmth blooming in her chest. Jay was right, life on the *Nanshe* is a million times better since she agreed to bring on a crew.

"One more thing," Lasadi says. "Ruby. I'm guessing you'll also want to scour the *Slingshot* for any info on your parents."

Ruby sits back slightly, worrying her lower lip with her teeth. "I was going to fit it in, yeah."

Since the very first job they pulled together, Lasadi has slowly been gaining an appreciation for the enormity of Ruby's task. In the inner planets, systems talk to each other, and a skilled hacker can skip from one to another in search of her prey. Out here, it's a patchwork of rumors and half-gathered information. Ruby's gathered pieces of the story on Auburn Station, through her searches in the Pearls, from the recesses of her memory, and by scouring the systems of Sapis Station. Lasadi's assumed she was planning to continue her search on the *Slingshot*, and she'd rather it be in the open rather than potentially put them all in danger, as had happened on Auburn Station.

More than that, Lasadi wants to help. And she wants Ruby to know she can confide in them all.

"Do it," Lasadi says, and Ruby's lips part in surprise. "And let us know what help you need."

"We'll need to get into Escat's system to break into his vault," Ruby says. "That should also get me the access I need to keep hunting. But I'll let you know if I run into any bumps."

"And let us know what you find." Lasadi takes a deep breath. "Everybody know what they need to work on? Then let's get to it."

CHAPTER 11
LASADI

LASADI STEPS THROUGH THE AIRLOCK TO THE *SLINGSHOT*'S marketplace unit, shaking off her disorientation. Guide lights and signage in the last few corridors have oriented "up" and "down" as being the same as a normal hallway despite the lack of gravity, but here in the marketplace, that orientation lurches ninety degrees. Lasadi's brain is telling her she should be entering at the far end of a long, wide chamber; instead, she's standing at the bottom of a six-story cylinder.

At least the designers have still given her an up and down to anchor herself to. She grew up with gravity and the expectation that down wouldn't change. It's how humans evolved, and despite the dozens of generations who've made their home in Durga's Belt, Lasadi can't help but think their genetic code is shouting for some sort of order.

It's why places like Auburn Station, deliberately built to keep people from finding spatial anchors, are the exception rather than the rule out here. Rasheda Auburn had been a belt drifter with a crew of other belt drifters from the beginning, and she knew the best way to throw her enemies off their game was to erase their sense of up and down.

The marketplace unit is much bigger than Lasadi had expected, despite having studied the plans. The curving walls are lined with stalls, some closed, others open and attended by humans, but most simply automated vending machines dispensing everything from groceries to spare parts. The middle area is taken up with a series of platforms attached to a central cable, each dotted with stasis fields to create common areas with tables where passengers can enjoy the food and beverages bought from merchants and vending machines.

There's no need for the platforms, of course. There will never be gravity on this part of the *Slingshot*. But it provides a nice illusion of normalcy and an organizing principle for the crowds.

Speaking of. A small one is already gathering at one of the middle platforms; Raj and Alex have been hard at work drumming up an audience.

"Karl Gatmaitan was in stall D9," Ruby says in Lasadi's ear. "To your right." Ruby's here already, too, inventorying the security and keeping an eye on Raj and Alex. "The shuttered stall next to the hottie in the yellow jumpsuit."

Letters indicating each row float in neon holograms up the wall, and Las doesn't need to count to find stall nine on row D — it's the only one shuttered. The stall to the right is an auto-vend, but the one on the left is staffed by a young person in a clean-but-fraying yellow flight suit, blond hair shaved close to reveal the tattoos on their scalp.

"I see it," Lasadi murmurs, unlocking her magboots and pushing off towards Gatmaitan's shuttered stall. "I'll try to round up some intel."

"You got your opening line ready?"

Lasadi frowns at Ruby's teasing tone. "Opening line? I

was thinking 'Did you know the man who ran the stall next door?'"

"Ah, the practical approach." Ruby laughs in her ear. "Personally I'd start by complimenting those sexy scalp tattoos."

"I'll leave that to you." Lasadi scans as she drifts, finally spotting Ruby on one of the lower platforms. Ruby's left her red leather jacket back on the *Nanshe* and is wearing a thin-strapped black tank top that shows off the golden tattoos of the Pearls across her collarbones. She winks at Lasadi and raises her bulb of coffee in a toast, then spins gracefully back to scanning the crowd.

Both of the Quiñones siblings are adept at maneuvering in zero G, moving with a finesse Lasadi can't quite match. Despite growing up in the gravity of Artemis City, Alex has the advantage of his acrobat's poise. And the flashes of childhood memory Ruby's started to recover since her run-in with Annika Lebedevya on Sapis confirm she'd spent the first twelve years of her life drifting through the Belt with her now-missing parents. That muscle memory is ingrained in her body from childhood.

The young vendor with the scalp tattoos has noticed Lasadi's approach and gives her a friendly smile. "You looking for hardware? Fasteners, safety equipment, hinges, rivets — I'm the woman to talk to."

Lasadi catches one of the rails outside the stall and brings herself to a gentle stop before locking her magboots to the grate outside the stall's door. A bright sign above reads Slingshot Hardware; the woman sees her noticing.

"Where you are, what you do," she says. "Everything you need in a business name."

"Straightforward." Lasadi holds out a hand. "I like it. I'm M.J."

"Fiona. What are you looking for, M.J.?"

"Actually, for the guy in stall D9. I met him on a run a

few years back and said I'd swing by if I was ever on the *Slingshot* again. Do you know when he'll be in?"

Fiona's bright smile falls. "Karl," she says sadly. "Afraid you missed him for good. He had a heart attack a month or so ago."

Lasadi feigns surprise. "I'm so sorry."

"Karl was a good guy. Weird one, but aren't we all out here?" A flash of a self-deprecating smile. "He always had a good story to tell, a joke and a laugh. And he was good for the community."

Something in the reverence Fiona gives that last word catches Lasadi's attention. "The community?" she asks. "I guess I think of the *Slingshot* as mostly just full of travelers."

"You're not from around here." Fiona's not asking; Lasadi has softened her Coruscan accent, but she doesn't have Raj's gift of tongues. She'll never sound like a local. "The *Slingshot* is the one place nearly everyone in the Belt comes through at one point or another. The *real* Belt, at least."

"Meaning, not the Pearls?"

"Nothing against the Pearls," Fiona says. "I'm not one of those Maribi Cartel assholes who think we'd be better off without the Federation. But it's a different breed who ride this boat out to find their fortune. We need to stick together, and Karl was a real help."

"A help with what?"

"Anyone who needed it. I run a community swap. Lots of people out here have a story where they only survived because some stranger gave them a hand. Lent them a spare part, or stopped for their distress call, or shared some rations. People are happy to donate what they don't need anymore, and I make sure it gets to the ones that do need it."

Fiona casts a dark look at the shuttered stall where Karl

Gatmaitan used to hawk his wares. "One of the ways Karl used to help was with storage," she says. "But when he died, they cleaned out his stall. I know it's in the contract, but the director wouldn't listen to me when I explained half of what was in there was donations."

"I hope it gets sorted out — surely the director will understand."

"Sure." Fiona's attention slips over Lasadi's shoulder, scanning for trouble. Her body language has tensed up, her jaw set and arms crossed.

"Is he not very understanding?"

"I'm more worried about his friends."

"What do you mean?" Lasadi asks, but Fiona gives her a false, tight smile. She has plenty to say, but she's not about to do it here.

"Well, I'm sorry to be the bearer of bad news," Fiona says, clearly changing the subject. "Karl was a good guy, but old age catches up to you quick out here."

"How long do you think his stall will stay empty?" Lasadi asks, following Fiona's lead to safe conversational ground. "Is there a lot of competition for the space?"

"Absolutely. None of these spots stay vacant for long. I just hope it's someone selling something people actually *need* rather than a huckster trying to make a quick buck." Fiona's gaze flicks to the gathering crowd above them. "Like that asshole."

Lasadi turns as Raj's voice sounds through the crowd he and Alex have whipped up around their demonstration. "Ian Chaulet at your service," he calls over the murmur. "Welcome to your future!"

Fiona's glare could cut glass. "People get desperate out here, start to look like prey, and the sharks start circling. Lots of folks selling miracles out here, not so many selling actual hope."

"That's awful." Lasadi hides her wince, holds out her hand. "Well, thank you for telling me about Karl."

"You're welcome," Fiona says; her hand is warm and grip is firm. "I'm sure I'll see you around. And you know where to come if you have extra supplies and want to pay it forward. Or if you need any help."

"Will do."

Lasadi releases her magboots and drifts on, pretending to peruse vendors until she finds Ruby positioned at the edge of the crowd where they can watch Raj at work.

"We might have a complication," Lasadi says. "I know our goal was to steal Gatmaitan's notes, but . . ."

"But how hard would it be to also lift the donations my new girlfriend Fiona was storing in his stall?" Ruby lifts an eyebrow; Lasadi nods. "No clue. I'll get back to you on that once Alex gets me into Escat's system."

"Thank you. And let's find out who Fiona meant by Escat's 'friends.'"

Ruby keeps scanning the room as Lasadi turns back to the show below them. Raj is in his element at the center of the gathering crowd, drawing them in with a sparkling eye and wide, friendly grin. He's too slick at this, Lasadi thinks. Good thing he has too much of a conscience to actually make a living as a con.

As Lasadi watches, Raj opens his hand with a flourish to reveal a small vial filled with glittering silver filings. The inner ring of spectators lean in, curious.

"Namidium," Raj says with reverence, and a murmur goes around the group. "Pure namidium."

"Let me see." A burly man shoulders his way to the inner circle around Raj, then unclips a scanner from his belt. He scans the vial and frowns at the reading on his heads-up display. "Impossible to tell." He hands the vial back to Raj. "I'd have to take it back to my lab."

"And therein lies the problem," Raj agrees. "Testing for

namidium is next to impossible in the field, which means entire rich veins of the stuff are going undiscovered. Possibly in claims you already are working." He pitches his voice so the crowd can hear it. "I'm not telling anything you don't already know. You've all suspected you could be extracting more value out of your mines, but you haven't been able to do anything about it. Until now."

A murmur around the group as Raj settles into the patter. Alex slips into the role of Raj's assistant easily, helping him demonstrate the traditional way of detecting rare metals in the asteroid mines against the new "tester" Ruby rigged up.

Lasadi deliberately found a spot out of sight of Fiona, but she can't help imagining how the other woman will be reacting to Raj's act. He's the perfect caricature of a get-rich-quick huckster, and while people are watching him warily, they're still listening. Folks out here have been sold plenty of shams before — only the newest adventurer on the *Slingshot* will be watching Raj's demonstration with stars in their eyes. But Fiona is right. People get desperate out in the black, and none of them are willing to turn away from the thing that might save them.

"Lots of folks selling miracles out here," Fiona had said. And it works, because there are so many people desperately in need of a miracle.

Raj is about to pass his demo apparatus on to the burly man who's been the most vocally suspicious when a shift in the crowd near the top of the marketplace catches Lasadi's attention. She nudges Ruby, who nods.

"Don't look, loves," she says into the comms. "But security's caught your scent. Above and on your left."

Raj dips his chin but otherwise doesn't respond, just keeps on with his patter as the security guards zero in on him, leaving a restless wake in the crowd as they pass. The guards are armored, with electric barbs prominent on their belts. Back in Artemis City their uniforms would look like riot gear and have the crowd's hackles up; here, the crowd doesn't seem bothered. No one's shrinking back, let alone moving out the way. At best, they're grudgingly deferential.

Lasadi forces herself to relax as one of the two armored figures drops a heavy hand on Raj's shoulder. If the *Slingshot*'s security guards were prone to unnecessary violence, the crowds would probably have reacted with more nervousness. Instead, they're dispersing with a mix of disappointed jeers at the guards and laughing catcalls at Raj.

"Can I see your permit?" the guard asks.

"Permit?" Raj motions for Alex to start packing things up. "I need a permit?"

"You'll need to come with us, sir."

Heavy hands clamp around Raj's arms, and the guard begins propelling him up to the top of the marketplace, Alex and the second guard on his heels.

Raj ghosts her a smile as they pass, and then they're gone through the top airlock of the marketplace.

"Perfect," says Ruby. "C'mon. Let's go see what intel they'll bring us."

CHAPTER 12
JAY

A QUICK SURVEY OF MODULE E's SHODDY SERVICES HUB MAKES Jay send up a prayer of thanks to the old ones that the *Nanshe* has its own showers and kitchen. The vending stall, kitchen station, recycling collector, and hygiene units are necessities for a lot of folks traveling through the black in tiny, ill-equipped ships. Even so, the kitchen's rehydrators are caked with grime, the recyclers overflowing, the hygiene units decidedly unhygienic looking. Everything from the stove to the shower is rentable by the quarter hour, prices scrawled on cracked signage beside the rusted doors, and a distinct bouquet of stale coffee, burnt plastic, and unwashed human — a mixture Jay has come to associate with the many deep-Belt dives he stayed in during the three years they worked for Nico Garnet — permeates the entire space. Charming.

Still. Some ships Jay saw docked alongside the *Nanshe* don't even offer room to stretch your legs. The chance to bathe and enjoy a different patch of wall for even a few minutes would be a luxury to some. Not to mention the opportunity to talk to someone who isn't inside your imagination.

The lounge area next to the kitchen is a slight improvement; it seems clean, if well-worn from years of use, and is comfortably occupied. One pair of travelers is arguing in one corner, sniping at each other over forkfuls of pale brown glop. A woman is reading at one of the tables, a bulb of beer floating next to her chair. Someone's snoozing on the far wall, arm looped through a tether and flask in their hand. And a trio are playing mystix around a stasis table that keeps glitching out; when it does, the players carefully hold their cards in place until it turns back on again.

Every head turns when he enters, except for the person with the flask, who lets out a tortured snore.

Jay gives a general nod to the group and heads to the vending stall, swipes through the options on the screen. The prices are higher than in the Pearls, but not by as much as he'd expect. The selection, on the other hand, is dismal.

Jay swipes credits off his gauntlet and jabs a finger at the button for Dolmara Gold, that ubiquitous shitty lager of the black. A door opens and a bulb appears. It's cold, at least; Jay cracks the seal and takes a pull of the weak brew as he scans his options for intel.

The arguing couple has gone back to bickering, the woman with the book has gone back to reading, the person with the flask remains insensible. Looks like he's playing mystix today. Jay catches the eye of the dealer, a slight woman with a mop of red hair.

"Mind if I buy in?"

"New money's always welcome," she says, and the other two players make space at the table.

"Just get in?" asks the man at the dealer's right. He's dark-skinned and clean-cut in a light gray suit; without the chipped tooth and scarred lip he could be an Ironfall banker.

"First time," offers Jay, and the man grins. "Hope it won't be the last."

"You don't look like a miner," says the woman at the dealer's left; she's lanky, with short black locs drifting around her round face.

"More of a trader," Jay says. "Thinking of opening up a stall, but heard it's hard to get a spot."

"You came at the right time, then," the woman with the locs says. "Old man Gatmaitan went static a few weeks back and his stall's still closed."

Old ones but Jay hates that particular bit of drifter slang. Conjures up too many memories. "That happen often? People . . . going static?"

"Depends on what you're selling," says the man with the chipped tooth, which earns him a steel-eyed glare from the dealer.

Jay glances between them. "Meaning?"

"Meaning it's smart to keep your tongue," says the dealer. "Are we playing or talking?"

She deals, and the little group plays without chatter for a moment, the only sound cards shuffling and the hushed argument from the couple in the corner. Jay's first few hands are mediocre — but so are everyone else's, poor draws that push credits back and forth between piles until the man with the chipped tooth goes all-in right after Jay's pulled a marriage of Nāga and Cave. Jay calls and reveals, the man with the chipped tooth groans and floats his pair of tens back to the dealer.

"I'm out," he says. "Y'all buy something nice with my credits."

"I'll be here tomorrow," says the dealer. "Same time."

The man laughs. "Don't I know it."

"Depends on what you're selling," he'd said in reference to Karl Gatmaitan's death before the dealer shut him down. Jay considers leaving the game himself to follow the man and ask what he meant, but that would be too obvious.

And it sounds like he's a regular at the mystix table. Jay can always try to hunt him down tomorrow.

People have been drifting through the hub as the last few hands played out, and now the dealer waves over a man who's been lurking near the vending machine. "Don't leave us shorthanded," she says with a grin. "I know you've got credits to lose."

The newcomer inclines his head to her, then settles into the place the man with the chipped tooth had been. He gives Jay a wary nod of greeting. He doesn't look like a belt drifter — or, he doesn't look like he's been a belt drifter long. Copper skin, round cheeks, dark beard close trimmed and neat, sharp hazel eyes. If he's staking his fortune on a mine, he hasn't let it dull his soul yet.

They play a few more rounds while bantering idly; the newcomer clearly is a regular in this part of the ship, but it doesn't seem like he's more than passing acquainted to either the dealer or the woman with the locs. Jay interjects rarely, minding his game and listening while credits slip back and forth across the table. Jay's next hand might have netted him something — the low run of hearts is strong on its own, but the woman with the locs voids him with a high marriage: Exiled Prince and Star. Jay swipes credits across with a good-natured curse. The dealer shuffles and begins the next round.

"So." The newcomer slides Jay a look. "What brings a Coruscan out to the black?"

He's clocked Jay's accent, but that doesn't mean much. He could be well traveled, he could have a Coruscan auntie, he could enjoy watching Coruscan dramas. Still, it's rarer than not that belt drifters *do* recognize Jay's accent. Not many Coruscans leave their moon, and few of those that do float this far away.

"Same thing as everyone," Jay says. "Fame and fortune."

"New face, same story." The newcomer glances at his cards and raises the bet. "Someone from the inner planets heard they could strike it rich in Durga's Belt and came to try their luck."

"Some of us do get lucky."

"And some of us are just trying to live." The smile on his lips when Jay calls his bet is sharp, turning to a scowl when he turns over a pair of fives and Jay flips sevens.

Jay sweeps up the credits. "I keep hearing there's plenty of room for someone to make their own luck in the Belt, no matter where they're from."

The newcomer doesn't respond.

Jay lets the next few hands loosen his shoulders, genuinely enjoying the game and the casual banter, despite the prickly newcomer. He has a mystix deck somewhere, having taken a liking to it in the CLA while passing evenings in the barracks with the rest of Mercury Squadron. He'd roped some of Nico Garnet's mercs into playing from time to time, and even did decently in a tournament in Ironfall last year, but he hasn't had time for regular games for a while.

Maybe he needs to dig the deck out and teach Alex to play. Start gambling for dishes duty with Raj and Ruby. He could probably even talk Las into joining, though she never had with Nico's mercs. She used to play with Mercury Squadron, though, back in the day. She used to do a lot of things then that she's finally starting to do again now. Like laugh.

Jay's luck runs strong a few more hands, and his pulse perks at the pair of high-numbered powers he's dealt to start the newest round: the Lorelei and the Leviathan. Drawing the three of blades does nothing to help, but his fourth draw is the Sea to pair with the Leviathan. Better would be the River to pair with the Lorelei — the highest marriage possible — but a lesser marriage and Lorelei high is still a damn good hand.

The newcomer studies Jay after he raises, then drums fingers on the table and calls. The dealer passes them both a fifth card.

Jay lets out a groan; the newcomer laughs, not unkindly.

"Every player knows that groan," he says. "You pulled a fortune killer. Either that, or you're bluffing."

"I'm too rusty to bluff." Jay lays his hand in the stasis field to show the Mirage he'd drawn, reversing the marriage advantage of Leviathan and Sea. The newcomer has no marriages, but he has the River Jay'd been hoping for. River high with his pair of nines and wandering Djinn tilt him over the edge.

"Good hand," says the newcomer. "Or it was before the Mirage."

"Happens."

"Maybe your luck's turned and it's time to head home, Coruscan."

Jay shrugs one shoulder. "Some of us don't have a home to go to."

This catches the newcomer's attention, earns Jay a deeper look. "You fought?"

"CLA." Jay pushes his cards back to the dealer and stands. Surprisingly, the newcomer does, too.

"Ah, c'mon, man," the dealer protests. "Keep that winning streak going."

"You know I prefer to quit while I'm ahead," the newcomer says. He lifts his chin to Jay. "Buy you a beer?"

Jay hesitates, considering. The man's been hostile to him all game, but this doesn't feel like a trap. Could be the barbs were his way of seeing if Jay was an outsider worth talking to. Could be he's one of those militant anti-Alliance types who idolize Corusca's failed stand. Could be he's running his own game and Jay seems like prey. Whatever his intentions, Jay wants information and conversation himself, which makes this a good match.

"Seems I already bought this round," he says. "I'm Jay."

The newcomer meets Jay's outstretched hand. "Malcolm." No surnames, this isn't that sort of place. "If you want something better than a Dolmara, follow me."

They head back down Module E's corridor past the *Nanshe*'s airlock to the services hub at the other end, where there's a real bar with a much nicer lounge. The other man orders a couple of beers from a bartender who clearly knows him, then points to a table in the corner. This place is a touch livelier than the shithole they just left, but there's still plenty of space for private conversation.

Malcolm clinks his bulb with Jay's. "Got off on the wrong foot, I think."

"I'm sure you see a lot of fortune hunters out here. I'd feel the same way if I was still back home watching Corusca get overrun."

"Lessens the sting when I win their credits." Malcolm's smile is friendly, now. "So. What's your story?"

"You probably heard it before. Grew up working class, joined the CLA when the Alliance started making things tight for folks like mine, came to the Pearls once the fight went bad. Now I'm looking for the next thing."

It's a mostly accurate timeline, though Jay's left off the three years they spent working for Nico Garnet — that's a debt he's happy to have paid and forgotten. He takes a sip of his beer; it's slightly better than the Dolmara Gold, but not by much. Little less of a petroleum aftertaste, at least.

"How about you? You grew up out here?"

The corner of Malcolm's lip twitches in the ghost of a smile. "Born and raised in the Belt. My family had a claim that got us by, but never landed the big fortune my folks had hoped for. Would've been enough, but when I was fifteen some asshole from one of the Pearls came out hunting for a good investment and talked my parents into signing away everything. By the time they realized they'd been had, they didn't have enough money to pay their way to another claim. They sent me to Maribi Station to work while they hunted down the next opportunity, but in the end, they didn't even have enough fuel to make it back. I didn't hear from them for years; someone finally found their ship drifting when I was seventeen."

"I'm sorry."

Malcolm shrugs, takes a pull on his beer as if to acknowledge that his story — like Jay's — is hardly unique.

"So, you're following in their footsteps?" Jay asks. "Working a claim of your own?"

"Not exactly. I'm not on the *Slingshot* for the lift, I'm here to help. A lot of vulnerable souls on this ship who could use someone looking out for them."

"You see a lot of people getting preyed on?"

"Every day."

"Then your goal's ambitious." Jay lifts an eyebrow. "Not a lot of money in that, is there?"

"I get by all right." The smile Malcolm turns on Jay holds secrets. "And I've had a bit more luck than my parents ever did."

More than all right, Jay would guess. Most of the other travelers Jay's seen on this boat have a hungry look to them. They're shabby and malnourished, their jumpsuits patched and repatched, their fingernails flaking, their cheeks hollow. Malcolm seems like he eats well enough, and his clothes are well-kept — almost new.

"People need someone to trust out here," Malcolm says. "Someone they know has their back."

"I thought that was the administration's job?"

"Escat?" Malcolm laughs. "He sees this boat as his private treasure chest. He's dipped his hand in a few too many times, though. People are starting to get angry."

"I heard he expects a payout if you strike it rich and want a ride back."

"Escat's playing with fire." Malcolm takes a sip of his beer. "Because he's fucking with the Belt. That's the beauty of this ship. It's the sole place in the Belt everyone comes through at one point or another — and we stick together." Malcolm seems about to say more, but his comm chimes and whatever he sees there sketches frown lines between his brows. "Speaking of, someone needs me." He flicks his contact information to Jay's comm. "We could use more good people. Keep in touch, friend."

"I'll catch you around."

"I'm sure you will."

Jay finishes his beer as he watches Malcolm leave, then floats their empties over to the bartender.

"Another?"

"No thanks." These bulbs are small, and the brews may not pack a punch, but he'll be ready for a nap if he has a third. He'll have plenty more work to do back at the *Nanshe* once Raj and Alex are done with their part of the plan. "You been working here long?"

"Long enough to remember when people cared for each other out here." The bartender says it with an air of well-worn complaint.

"Yeah?"

"Back when I was a kid, folks could make a living off a mine, or join up with one of the collectives. Now with the Alliance corporations, it's cutthroat. People don't trust each other anymore. Every kid still thinks they can come out here and strike it rich, then head back to Artemis City to buy a townhouse."

"Kids like Malcolm?" Jay tilts his chin at the door Malcolm exited through.

The bartender shakes his head. "He's one of the helpers."

"Like that vendor who died recently," Jay says. "I heard about that — it's the old guard, right? They don't make them like they used to."

The bartender shifts, expression suddenly guarded. "He caught what's been going around," he says carefully.

Jay frowns at him. "Heart attacks are contagious?"

"Greed is. Good luck out there." And he returns to his work, his back to Jay.

The place between Jay's shoulder blades itches, and he turns to scan the room. Is it his imagination, or did he catch the other patrons suddenly looking away? The music in the bar suddenly seems too loud, the stench of disinfectant and booze too strong; Jay's definitely ready to be back on the *Nanshe*.

"He caught what's been going around."

What the hell is that supposed to mean?

CHAPTER 13
RAJ

RAJ HAS ALWAYS BEEN FASCINATED BY THE WAY PEOPLE DISPLAY wealth in Durga's Belt, so different from what he saw growing up in Arquelle. Indicators of wealth back home tended to be stately and refined, with an old money culture that came with its own sets of unwritten rules. Arquelle was one of the first places humans settled in the Durga System, but it's not only that. People have been living in Durga's Belt for centuries, but even the wealthiest are still fairly transient, and generational wealth is rarer than not.

Life here is dangerous, and wealth displays are flashy. Few worry about investing for the future or leaving a legacy; it makes more sense to spend what you have now and make some more later when you need it — or assume you'll be dead by the time the debt comes due.

If there was any doubt in Raj's mind that Director Daniel Escat was successful, the flash on display in his office proves he is. And that he wants the world to know it. Excellent. They can use that.

Escat extends a hand when Raj and Alex are escorted in, greeting them both with a smile. He's balding, with silver hair shorn close and deep furrows around his mouth and between his eyes that deepen when his smile broadens. Not the arrogantly controlling dictator Raj's father had been, but there's still steel in the handshake. Escat's friendliness covers a hard edge. Raj files that away.

"Welcome to my humble office." Escat directs Raj and Alex to sit in the trio of comfortable chairs around a stylish coffee table. It's equipped with a stasis field, but it's not currently turned on. Doesn't need to be. One of the many luxuries Escat has procured for himself is artificial gravity in his personal module.

It will pose an unexpected challenge when it comes to breaking into his storage unit, but that's not Raj's problem. Alex is already testing his weight, bouncing on the balls of his feet like an excited child as soon as they entered the module. He'll be noting the security features and layout, too, filing every detail away into that terrifying memory of his.

Raj sits, setting the bag containing Ruby's "namidium tester" and samples at his feet. Escat joins him, but Alex stops to admire a wall hanging, eyes wide.

"The colors in this are amazing!" Alex brushes a finger over the fibers. "Where'd you get it?"

Perfect; Alex is a natural, and that was the exact right question to ask. Every surface of Escat's office is covered by art and trinkets. Random pieces that bring him joy? Mementos? Pieces he collected because of their value? Whatever the reason, getting Escat talking about the art will teach Raj a lot about how to play this man.

"A gift from a family from Xichin Station." Escat seems surprised by Alex's question, but he's obviously delighted to be asked. A collector who's proud to talk about his trophies, Raj notes. "A token of thanks on their way home from a successful haul I counseled them about."

Token of thanks. A rather polite term for extortion, if the rumors are true.

"Really?" Alex keeps his smile broad. "Wow."

Raj clears his throat to get Escat's attention while Alex moves to another piece of art. "Mr. Escat, I want to apologize for our little show down in the market. We knew you needed a permit to sell, but I didn't realize I'd need one for a demonstration."

"Quite all right, Mr. . . ."

"Chaulet. Ian Chaulet. And this is my overly inquisitive assistant, Jonas." He shoots Alex a faux glare; the kid ignores him.

"Quite all right, Mr. Chaulet. You'll understand why we need to vet demonstrations like yours. Passengers on the *Slingshot* are a captive audience, and when people take advantage of that, it can make for a frustrating experience. My goal is to make the trip as pleasant as possible. And that means curbing ad hoc hawking."

Escat smiles smugly at the turn of phrase. Someone who enjoys making jokes he thinks will go above his audience's head. Raj files that away, too.

"Mr. Escat, I keep hearing — "

"Wow, this view!"

Escat and Raj both turn to find Alex with his nose pressed against a porthole. Alex turns back with a grin. "You must be the only one on the ship with a view like this."

"Not the only one," Escat allows. "The cabins in Module C all have portholes, and the view from the lounge there is spectacular."

The first-class cabins and lounge, Escat means, though he'd avoided calling the class difference out. Politeness? Diplomacy? A desire to pretend that everyone on the *Slingshot* travels as equals, though that's obviously far from the case?

"Mr. Escat," Raj says, and the director's attention shifts away from Alex once more. "I keep hearing you're the man to talk to about mining claims. The man with the golden touch."

"I have had a bit of luck with my investments." Escat seems accustomed to flattery. He has ego, which Raj can use, but he's not the kind of man who will bluster blindly after a compliment.

"Then talking with you will be a good litmus test of how useful my product actually is."

"Namidium testing." Escat's fingers drum on his thigh; he's interested, but not going to say it outright.

Most of the people who saw Raj's earlier demonstration in the marketplace are gamblers — that's the nature of a gold rush. Do your research (or not), stake a claim (or steal one), and hope what you find pays for the investment in time and resources it took you to scrape everything of value out of the veins of the asteroid. But Escat isn't a miner. He's an investor. Someone who makes smart decisions with as much information as possible and only goes after what he considers to be sure deals.

"What if you could stop gambling, and start knowing for certain if a claim had namidium? Or?" Raj leans in. "Squeeze even more profits out of a claim you already own?"

Escat's attention, which has been flitting back and forth between Raj and Alex as Alex admires the rest of the artwork, is entirely on Raj now.

"I watched your demonstration over the video feeds," he says. "I heard your outrageous assertions. May I look at the device?"

"Of course." Raj unwraps the detector and sets it on the coffee table. Escat turns suddenly back to Alex. Raj tenses, but Escat doesn't seem to notice Alex fixing a bug behind a framed portrait of an old woman done in a post-precision revival style. The dark, bold lines around the eyes means it's probably an é Khatib, or one of her students.

His mother would be proud he remembers. Before his father had put a stop to them, art lessons with her were one of Raj's favorite subjects.

An old wound, but it still aches; Raj shakes off the memory as Escat motions to Alex.

"Young man, can you bring me some samples? They're behind my desk. Three of them: the large rock with the silver flecks, the bluish one to its right, and the green one at the far left."

"You got it."

A stasis field against the wall holds a number of rocks, and the fact that the field is turned on means the artificial gravity must not be constant. Raj files that away as well. Alex plucks the rocks Escat asked for out of the stasis field and tosses them underhand to Raj — another test of the gravity — then leans in to admire the other samples in the collection. "Is this real gold?"

"It is, another gift from a different family I helped years ago." Escat's attention shifts off Alex once more and returns to the silver-flecked stone Raj hands him. Raj pins Alex with a *Don't you dare steal that gold* look, then begins to lead Escat through a demonstration of the device. He sticks with the patter Ruby taught him, mostly, embellishing from time to time to keep Escat's attention captive.

"And if you'll do the honors?" Raj presents Escat with the device, now loaded with the sample of the silver-flecked stone. Escat presses the button with a dubious expression. His lips purse a touch, satisfied, when the device flickers to green; he's not surprised to see the sample contains namidium.

The device turns red when they load the bluish stone into the sample slot, then green again for the final sample. Escat makes a small sound of surprise.

"You knew the first sample had namidium in it, right?"

Raj asks; Escat nods. "You might want to take another look at the mine where you got the third sample."

"I might do that," Escat says.

Alex drops into the chair beside Raj's, having completed his tour of the office artwork — and his part of the job. He grins at Escat. "With this technology, everyone will be taking another look at their mines."

"Hmm." A muscle jumps in Escat's jaw as he considers the device, turning the third sample over in his fingers. For a man who seems to pride himself on helping others, the idea of making this technology widely available doesn't seem to sit well. Of course, Escat's built up his reputation and fortune by positioning himself as the person others come to for advice and information. Raj can see him wondering why he shouldn't be the person they come to for namidium testing, too.

A knock at the door jolts Escat out of his musings, and the door slides open. "He's here to see you," says a young man.

Escat's nostrils flare. Annoyance at the interruption? Wariness at whoever has arrived? "Tell him I'll be a moment."

When the aide disappears, Escat gives Raj an apologetic smile. But it no longer reaches his eyes, and he's unconsciously twisting the ring on his right hand. Something about this next appointment has him on edge.

"I'm afraid this conversation will have to continue another time, gentlemen," Escat says. "Please refrain from any more demonstrations — public or private — until we can speak more."

"Until we get that permit?" Raj asks.

"Or we could set up a stall," Alex says. "I noticed one was empty. Some old guy died of a heart attack?"

Something flashes across Escat's face — guilt? Certainly recognition; he knows who Karl Gatmaitan was, and that there's more to the story than the official version. Escat turns the final sample stone over in his fingers, studying the surface with a new appreciation.

"I may have a more interesting offer for you than a permit or a stall," he says, then glances at the door. "A partnership."

"I'm not sure we need a partner," Raj says; irritation flashes in Escat's eyes before he smooths his expression into a friendly one once more.

"You may change your mind once you see my offer," Escat says. "Remember. Don't speak of this to anyone else, even if they approach you. I'll be in touch."

Raj scans the antechamber of Escat's office when they leave, but he doesn't see who might be waiting for Escat. Not a problem, though. Not if Alex did his job.

"Ruby," he murmurs once they're out of the director's module. "You in?"

"I'm in," she says in his ear. "Meet you back at the *Nanshe*."

CHAPTER 14
LASADI

TONIGHT JAY'S FILLED THE *NANSHE*'S LITTLE GALLEY WITH THE heavenly scent of garlic and vegetable stir-fry, and every bite Lasadi takes is divine.

"I've never fallen in love with a man before," Ruby says around a mouthful of rice. "But if you keep cooking like this I might make an exception." Jay returns her smile, but his comes a second too slow; something's been bothering him since they all returned to the *Nanshe* and Lasadi hasn't had a chance to ask what it is.

"Can't wait to see what you cook when it's your day," he teases.

"Mmm-hmm." Ruby shakes her head. "About that. I nominate Jay as head chef."

"Seconded." Lasadi pops a piece of carrot in her mouth. "I don't think any of you want my cooking."

"Don't sell yourself short," Jay says. "I've seen you rehydrate TVP curry with the best of them."

"My point exactly."

"I can cook!" Alex says. He plucks one the bulbs of hot sauce — Jupari Sunset — from the rack behind him.

Ruby eyes him suspiciously. "Since when."

"I helped the ayas in the kitchen a lot."

"As punishment for some insane stunt, love?"

"The *why* doesn't matter," Alex says breezily. He recaps the hot sauce and floats it across the table to Lasadi. "The important thing is I actually *do* know how to cook. Aya Julio taught me."

"Then you're up next," Lasadi says, catching the hot sauce bulb.

"I'll see if I can procure some garbanzo beans," Alex says.

"Pay for them, please." Lasadi holds his gaze until Alex shrugs like *Of course, why wouldn't I?* "We have plenty for you to steal already. The last thing we need is to get stung because you've got sticky fingers."

"I would never, Cap. There was all sorts of shiny gold in Escat's office and I left it entirely alone."

"He did," confirms Raj. "I triple-checked."

"Glad to hear it. Speaking of theft, how are we shaping up?"

"We've a good start," Ruby says. "Alex bugged Escat's office and got me into his system, and now I have everything we need to break into his storage unit — access codes, schedules, schematics. Twist is we'd planned to send Alex in for Karl Gatmaitan's notes, only. I'll need a bit more time if we're also going to steal back the donations Gatmaitan's cute neighbor with the scalp tattoos collected."

"Start working on it," Lasadi says. "But don't make any moves yet. We have to time this right before we leave."

"Alex also cloned a private data cube from Escat's desk," Ruby says. "I've got a lockpick script running on it now — doesn't hurt to have more intel."

"What I want to know is who Escat met with after Alex and me," Raj says. He scoops another helping of stir-fried vegetables into his bowl, shakes his head when Lasadi offers him the bulb of Jupari Sunset. "Ruby, can you see who it was? I got the impression Escat wasn't delighted."

Ruby swipes at her tablet, then frowns. "Nothing," she says. "And nothing on Escat's official calendar. Maybe the appointment didn't actually show."

"Or maybe they used a scrambler shield."

"Possible. I'll let you know if there are any other mysterious blank spots in the data."

"Check the passenger list, too," Raj says. "Escat's built up quite the little empire for himself and he seemed extremely comfortable on his throne — until we were interrupted. Somebody's threatening his security."

"Someone from the Pearls Federation, maybe," Ruby says. "If he's overstepped his bounds one too many times."

"Maybe," Lasadi says. "But your girlfriend Fiona said she was more worried about Escat's friends than Escat. Doesn't sound like the Federation to me."

"Could be someone local," Jay says. "The guy I met, Malcolm? He told me Escat was playing with fire because he was messing with people in the Belt."

"Plenty of nasties out here for Escat to tangle with," Ruby says. "Half the local stations are run by cartels and the other half are infested with pirates."

"Spoken like a true Artemisian," Lasadi teases.

"Fine, fine," Ruby says with an eye roll. "There are decent pockets outside of the Pearls. But you'll admit the *Slingshot* goes through some shady bits of the Belt."

Lasadi nods, conceding the point. "Jay, see if you can get in touch with Malcolm again. Find out what he meant. Raj, where did you leave things with Escat?"

"He seemed interested in the prototype," Raj says. "He wants to make us an exclusive offer — he seemed upset I wouldn't consider it, and he'll be disappointed when we disappear into the night without selling it to him. Ruby, do you think you could get this thing working for real?"

"Who are you talking to, love. I've been thinking it through, and — "

"Hold on," Lasadi says. "We're here for Karl Gatmaitan's notes, not to make money off Escat. Your ruse got us into the office, but don't overplay the hand."

"A thought experiment," Raj says with a smile.

Ruby shrugs. "And if I did get it working, we wouldn't sell it to Escat, would we. My girlfriend Fiona could help a lot of people with this tech."

"Or it might put her in the crosshairs," Jay says. While the rest of them have been devouring dinner, he's been picking at his food.

Ruby's eyebrows shoot up. "Crosshairs?"

"It could be nothing." Jay scrubs a hand over his chin. "Did some digging while the rest of you were out. Conversation came around to Gatmaitan's death and the vibe got strange. I asked if it happened often that people died on the *Slingshot*, and someone said, 'It depends on what you're selling.' The others shut him down. Later, a bartender told me Gatmaitan 'caught what's been going around.' Wouldn't say anything more. We should look into it."

"If it becomes our business, absolutely," Lasadi answers.

Jay flicks her a look. "Lotta people on the *Slingshot* just trying to make a living and need protection. It's pretty clear Escat's preying on them, yeah?"

"It's all he could talk about," Alex says around a mouthful of hot sauce–soaked rice. Sweat beads on his dark brow. "His office was packed with 'gifts' he got from people he claims he helped."

"Then we should do something more than grab Gatmaitan's notes and go," Jay says.

Lasadi studies him; she can't read the reason behind the serious set of his jaw, the intensity in his eye, but she can tell it's important. "Fine," she says after a moment. "Ruby, see if you can find patterns in anyone who died out here in the last few years. The rest of you, keep an ear out. If we find anything, we can decide together what to do next. Alex? Talk us through your plan for getting into the director's module."

Jay vanished after dinner as the others joined in cleanup, giving an excuse about the *Nanshe*'s engine and shutting down Lasadi's attempt to follow him. He's in one of his quiet moods; she could hound him until he shares whatever's bothering him, or she could let him work through it on his own until he's processed what he needs to and is ready to tell her.

Some people think best out loud — Ruby and Raj's constant banter during dinner cleanup puts them squarely in that category. Jay, on the other hand, has always retreated into silence with his thoughts when pondering something difficult. He'll come to her when he's ready.

Galley tidied, Ruby vanishes into her room to check her bugs and continue her search. Alex heads to his own a few minutes later, and Lasadi should take care of some messages — Tora Garnet has pinged her again, with a more direct command: Call me.

Lasadi secures the last of the dishes in their storage cupboard with a wince. She stretches her neck and rolls her shoulder, trying to ease the sharp pinch between her shoulder blades that's been growing all evening. Something about the way she slept last night, maybe, or the tension of this trip. That nerve flares up sometimes on long trips in zero G — it's one of the milder gifts the Battle of Tannis left her with.

She turns back to find Raj watching, and gives him a weary smile.

"My shoulder bothers me sometimes on long flights," she says. "Nothing a good night's sleep can't fix."

"Or a massage?" Raj asks; Lasadi stills. "I've been told I'm pretty good."

"It's fine." She dials her smile a touch brighter in an attempt to cover whatever panic had appeared in her eyes, then sits across from him, putting the length of the table between them as if that will keep her from giving in. "It's late."

Raj leans on his elbows, hands folded lightly on the table in front of him. A stray strand of hair has escaped from his ponytail and is brushing his cheek. She can't quite parse his expression, but it's a mix of compassion, curiosity, and heat. He's trying to decide if he should let it go, she thinks. If she tells him *No, not tonight,* she knows he won't press. He'll give her a smile. He'll bid her good night like always. They'll go to their separate rooms, as they probably ought to, here in the middle of a job.

She opens her mouth to say the words, but he speaks first.

"Do you not want a massage?" he asks quietly. "Or do you not want me to see your scars again."

The pain beside her shoulder blade stabs when she takes a quick breath; Lasadi makes herself relax, tries to force the tension out of her body. Around them, the ship has gone quiet: soft hum of life support systems, rush of water through pipes on the cargo deck indicating Jay is still up, though the others are in their own rooms with the doors closed.

Still, Lasadi pitches her voice low.

"What's the first thing you thought, when you saw them?"

Raj's eyes widen in surprise at the question, then narrow in thought, his gaze never leaving hers; he's considering his words carefully. "How lucky I am," he finally says. He clears his throat. "What I mean is, both of us had moments in our lives where things could have gone very differently. I know that. But I didn't actually know how close I'd come to never meeting you in the first place. I saw your scars and was intensely grateful to whatever power in the universe brought you through that fire to me."

Lasadi stares at him, unsure how to respond. It's not remotely what she'd been expecting him to say.

"What do you see?" he asks gently.

"It's not what I see, it's what I hear." Lasadi swallows, forcing herself to put words to the roiling lurch she feels every time she catches a glimpse of herself in a mirror. "I hear the voices of everyone under my command, vanishing one at a time. Jay screaming my name — I figured that would be the last thing I ever heard." She realizes her hands are clasped tight, nails digging into tender flesh; she forces them flat on the table. "I wasn't supposed to make it through that."

Raj's answer is to stand, circling the table to close the distance between them. His hand is warm on her shoulder as he steps behind her chair, lips brushing a kiss below her right ear.

"You were," he murmurs, the words a gentle hum against her neck.

Lasadi takes a deep breath, filling her lungs with Raj's citrus and salt. "I was," she finally agrees. Whatever chapter of her life had been cut short over Tannis, she'd survived it to begin writing a new one together with the *Nanshe*'s new crew. She lets her breath out slow, the needle of pain in her shoulder blade melting as the pad of Raj's thumb begins to trace strong lines down the muscle.

"So," he murmurs. "Did you want that massage?"

"Yes." She turns, breaking his touch. "Only — "

"I kept one of Absolon's privacy shields." Mischief

lights up Raj's eyes. "Thought it might come in handy, the tight quarters of the ship and all."

Lasadi laughs. "Then, yes."

She doesn't stand to lead them to her cabin, though, not right away. She's enjoying the way Raj's fingers tease into the stiff muscle of her shoulders too much to let him stop. She doesn't flinch when he pulls back the collar of her shirt. Doesn't flinch when his fingers begin to knead the taut expanse of scar tissue on her left shoulder. She'd been told by the doctors regular massage would be helpful to break the scar tissue down, but at the time it had seemed like such a lost cause. She'd thought nothing would make her body whole again — and maybe nothing ever will. But that's starting to matter less and less.

She's fully relaxed when his fingers still, drifting away from her shoulder. "Why don't you grab that privacy shield?" she murmurs through a glow of contentment.

Raj doesn't respond.

Lasadi swivels on her stool, curious, to find his eyes closed, lashes fluttering violently. Icy fear shoots through her.

"Raj?" She gets to her feet, ignoring the wave of dizziness that crashes into her. His breath is coming labored, and through her swimming vision she can see flecks of foam on his lips. "Help!" she yells. "We need help!"

But her own world is shrinking. Her nostrils burn at the unfamiliar bite in the air, her tongue tastes sharp and metallic and wrong.

She reaches for Raj as the world goes black.

CHAPTER 15
JAY

Jay was too wired to try to sleep, but that's what makes having a berth next to the engine room so perfect. Nothing like an hour losing himself in familiar kafusa beats and the comfort of his never-ending list of repairs to get his mind calm again.

Tonight it's not working.

He's frustrated with Las, and he's still trying to figure out exactly why. He'd told her they needed to investigate, and she'd agreed with him — eventually. But he can tell she'll drop it the instant he stops pushing, and he's not sure how to articulate that this is important. The more he worries at the moment, the more he's forced to realize that a tension with her has been growing inside him, a sick feeling in the pit of his stomach he's been trying to ignore. For how long?

He's always prided himself on being easygoing, on not much caring what direction he's going so long as he's with the people he loves. He knows this means he can't always tell the difference between what he wants and what he thinks others want; sometimes by the time he realizes there's a disconnect, it feels impossible to trace it back to its roots.

Ingrained habits from growing up with two older sisters, maybe. Both were headstrong and stubborn and always at odds — as the youngest child he'd either been the peacemaker or been ignored until the day he was finally pushed far enough to articulate something else that had been needling at him for years.

He'd been ten, his mother come home from shopping with three matching frilly dresses for Jay's father's swearing-in ceremony as union president. She'd spent far more than they could afford, but the formal occasion demanded something nice — and Jay had refused to put the dress on.

He'd struggled to articulate why with the same sick feeling currently churning in his stomach, that feeling he now recognizes means he's fundamentally opposed to what someone he loves wants him to do. His mother hadn't listened to what he'd faltered to say — her mind was caught in the panic of a dwindling bank account, and all she'd heard was she'd spent money they couldn't afford and her normally easygoing child wanted to throw it away.

She'd started to shut down the conversation, but Jay's father leaned forward, a hand on hers.

"Wait," he said, frown deepening as he began to understand that Jay's sudden stubborn streak was more than a whim, that this conversation was about so much more than a dress. "What are you trying to say?"

"I'm a boy."

Jay had finally forced the words out through an aching jaw, and his mother's eyes flashed wide, the room gone silent but for the sound of Jay's heart slamming in his ears.

Then his father barked out a laugh, grabbed Jay's shoulders with work-calloused hands, and kissed the top of his head.

"What have I been saying," he murmured to his wife,

voice gruff with emotion and pride, and he carefully picked up the discarded dress, smoothing the pleats back into the box with rough fingertips indelibly stained with grease. "I'll return this. Come on, son. Let's go shopping."

Jay's easygoing until he's pushed too far out of alignment, and something about this job has him tense. Something about the way Las seems content to ignore the suffering surrounding them these days, when the woman he'd followed into battle had been incandescent with her desire to make the world a better place.

He turns a wrench, the churning in his gut replaced now by an uneasy alliance of conviction and dread at the conversation he and Las need to have. He takes a deep breath, trying to organize what he'll say to her, then pauses. Replaces the wrench in the stasis field and cuts the music in his headphones before he even realizes he's going to do it.

Something has caught his attention, some instinct flashing his thoughts from muddled to crystal clear in a heartbeat. Jay sits back, all senses attuned to the ship around him.

Lasadi's voice comes again — he can't make out the words, but the panic in her tone is electric. She's still on the deck above him, it sounds like. Jay pushes himself up.

And stills, because something's very wrong. A wave of dizziness hits him like a fist, a faint burning stench filling his nostrils.

Jay's father had always insisted on carrying an emergency depressurization mask in his toolkit, no matter whether he was working near Corusca's surface or not, and Jay has kept up the habit. Jay launches himself across the engine room to the blue-and-gray duffel secured inside the door, holding his breath and narrowing his focus on keeping his movements smooth, his panic down. Nothing to be gained by flailing but jammed zippers and lost precious seconds.

The burning scent in his nostrils intensifies — as does the desperation in his lungs — and finally Jay's fingers close around the foil packet at the bottom of his bag.

Should be keeping it in an outer pocket, he can hear his dad saying.

Sorry, Pops.

Jay tears the packet open and slips the mask over his face, taking a deep, grateful breath as the seal catches and oxygen begins to flow.

Something's gone wrong with the *Nanshe*'s atmospheric system, and Jay's been through enough drills with his father and the CLA to know exactly what it is. And how little time he has to fix it.

He scans into the terminal in the engine room, still concentrating on keeping his breath measured and movements smooth as he navigates to the emergency atmosphere flush. He can't do a full vent — Las and the others were going to bed, he can't assume they realized what was happening in time to find an emergency DP mask like he had. But the *Nanshe*'s ventilation system is powerful, and a breeze brushes the exposed skin on the back of his neck as the system pumps fresh air in and vents the poison.

Because they've been poisoned. It's clear as day on the diagnostics console. A malfunction in the way the *Nanshe*'s system connected to the *Slingshot*'s caused it to overproduce the wrong atmospheric chemicals and create a toxic brew inside the ship. Jay's been taught to recognize the problem, but he's never heard of it actually happening. Not in his generation, at least, or even his father's. Today's ships have mandatory failsafes to prevent the sort of deadly tragedy that used to be more common when humans first set out to colonize Durga's Belt.

The *Nanshe* definitely has the right failsafes, and no one on this ship has the access to override it besides him and Lasadi. And even if another crew member did have access, the failsafes are buried under too many layers of security and confirmation to get turned off by accident.

Which means someone did this on purpose.

Jay waits a few seconds more to make sure the system is doing its work — the toxicity levels dropping — before he grabs the emergency med kit from his duffel and pushes himself out of the engine room and up the hatch to the crew level.

Las and Raj are in the galley. Raj's eyes are closed but he's breathing in ragged gasps, lungs pulling at the fresh air. Lasadi's eyes are bloodshot but she's awake and reaching for Raj.

"Ruby and Alex," she pants when she spots Jay.

Jay spins to face Ruby's room as her door opens. She's dressed in blue lumosilk pajamas, hair braided, one hand clawing the edge of her door, the other clutching her own emergency mask to her face.

Jay launches himself for Alex's door.

The kid is cozy in his bunk, a tablet drifting from his outstretched hand, that game he's gotten hooked on still chiming cheerful plinks and beeps from the screen. His eyelashes are fluttering. His lips are blue.

Jay tears the emergency DP mask off his own face and slips it over Alex's, pulling down the collar of his cotton undershirt to check his pulse. Faint; Alex's chest rasps under Jay's hand.

He hears Ruby cry out behind him, feels her join him beside the cot. She's already tearing at the med kit Jay brought with him.

"ReSat," Jay says, and a second later she slaps the oxygen resaturation kit into his palm. Jay slaps the injector against Alex's neck and hears the satisfying hiss, feels the smoothing of Alex's breath, the strengthening of his heartbeat.

Alex's eyes flash open, then slowly close again — the

ReSat's sedatives work alongside the hyperoxygenated nanites to make sure the patient doesn't panic themselves into undoing the good work of resaturating their blood with oxygen after an atmospheric poisoning or depressurization accident.

"Is it working?" Ruby asks.

"Yeah." Jay's never used one before himself, but he's seen them used more than once, and this looks right. When he presses Alex's outstretched finger into the oximeter, the readings are climbing. He lets his shoulders relax. "It's working."

Ruby smooths shaking fingers over Alex's freckled forehead, tracing constellations that mirror the ones on her own dark cheeks. "What the fuck happened."

"Someone sabotaged us," Jay says quietly. "And you and I are going to figure out who — after we get your brother to the medbay."

Ruby's nostrils flare with fury, and together they unstrap Alex from his cot and float him through the door. Las has regained her color in the scant minutes since Jay saw her last, and Raj is awake once more. His face is ashen, but he straightens when he sees the others.

"Alex — "

"He'll be okay," Jay says quickly — it has to be true, he's seen ReSats bring people back from far deeper cases. "We got to him fast. You two?"

"All good," Las says. "What happened?"

Ruby takes Alex's shoulders, guiding him towards the medbay door. "I've got him," she says. "But talk loud, will you, because if I'm going to murder a bastard, I need to know who."

Jay positions himself at the aft end of the galley nearest the medbay, so Ruby can hear him as she works with the medbay door open. He explains what happened as clearly as possible: the failsafes, the systems communication issue, the toxic poison that ended up releasing into the *Nanshe*.

"Awfully archaic way to die, isn't it?" Raj says. "I remember reading about it in the officer's academy."

"Happens more than you'd think out here," Ruby says from the medbay. "Two to three times a year out in the ass-end of the Belt where they're using older tech. Shouldn't be a problem with the *Nanshe*, though."

Of course Ruby'd be well versed in the many ways to die in the black. She may not talk about it much, but you can't spend this much time on a ship with someone who's terrified of death by vacuum without getting that message loud and clear. No wonder she'd been the other crew member who had an emergency DP mask handy at her bunk; her paranoia probably saved her from getting as strong a dose as her brother.

"It couldn't have happened on the *Nanshe*," Jay confirms. "Even in the ass-end of the black. I barely glanced at the diagnostics before I hit the emergency protocols, but the only way to get a malfunction like that is if someone overrides the failsafes at a core level. Only Las and I have that kind of access."

"Well, I didn't do it," says Lasadi. "And I assume you didn't."

"And obviously Ruby didn't do it," Raj says.

"Course I didn't, did I."

Jay glances over his shoulder; Ruby's got her brother strapped into the autodoc chair. She looks chagrined when she meets his eyes.

"You have core access to the *Nanshe*," Jay says, understanding.

"Olds." Lasadi sighs. "For how long, Ruby."

Jay lifts an eyebrow. "Since she first got on the ship, I assume."

"I haven't gone in since that first day," protests Ruby.

"Loves, I can't help breaking into systems, but I swear to the saints I haven't touched a thing or read any private communications. I just needed to know we were safe."

Lasadi sighs. "Maybe you can use your criminal compulsions to strengthen my ship's security so no one else can ghost in?"

"I already did, Cap." Her lips thin. "Or, at least I thought I had."

"Someone still got in," Jay says. "And we'll figure out who."

"And saints help them when we find them." Ruby's gaze is hard and sharp as steel. A chill traces down Jay's spine: If he'd been asleep instead of tinkering, they'd all be dead. Whoever's responsible for this will pay.

CHAPTER 16
LASADI

IT'S WELL AFTER MIDNIGHT LOCAL TIME WHEN THE CREW finally reconvenes in the galley to share what they've found. Lasadi scans their faces; everyone looks as tired as she feels. The autodoc cleared Alex a few minutes ago and now his color is good, though there are bloody threads in his sclera and a dull purple bruise on his neck from the ReSat kit. Still, he looks plucky as ever. Maybe he doesn't realize he nearly died — or maybe he doesn't believe in death yet.

Ah, to be seventeen again.

The adrenaline and fury that fueled Lasadi's past few hours is ebbing, replaced by a dull exhaustion. The pinched nerve in her shoulder is agony when she moves wrong — getting to finish that massage would have been nice. But it would have been even nicer if someone hadn't broken into her ship's system and tried to murder her entire crew.

The possessive ember that's been flickering inside her chest for the past few weeks has burst into pure, strong flame. She cannot let this happen again.

"So." Lasadi lets out a long breath. "Who tampered with the system?"

"Director Escat," answers Raj without hesitation.

"We don't know that for sure," points out Ruby. "But I'd put credits on it."

"And what did he" — Lasadi shoots Raj a look — "or whoever it was do?"

"It was buried deep, but I found it," Ruby says. "Someone sent a flea in on the *Slingshot*'s handshake code."

"Handshake code?" asks Alex.

Ruby nods. "It's like an information exchange. Makes sure the systems are compatible before docking and creates a protective layer where both ships can interface without danger. It's supposed to prevent this sort of thing, but this code had a flea that burrowed into our core systems, allowing outside override access. I trapped it in a construct that's isolated from the *Nanshe*'s systems, then flushed and resecured everything. It can't happen again."

"Which means whoever did this knows by now they failed," says Lasadi; Ruby nods. "The flea on the handshake code — why didn't our system detect it?"

"It was brilliant, only. Handshake codes vary a bit, but most governments or agencies have a standard they use across all their locations. For example, Alliance ships and stations all have their own code. So will any ships or stations administered by the Federation. I compared the *Slingshot*'s code to the code the *Nanshe* has stored from the docks in Artemis City and Ironfall, and everything is Federation standard. Except for one bit in the medcheck request."

"Medcheck?" Alex asks. "Like, asking for our medical history?"

"It gets nonidentifying data from the autodocs," says Lasadi. She knows about the medcheck requests; back when she first started doing runs on the *Nanshe* for Nico, she'd made sure the data was locked down as tight as legally possible to ensure she was compliant while remaining safely dead. The other option was never using the autodoc, and she'd had too many health complications in those early days to risk that. "They're meant to screen anyone who's showing signs of viral infection and needs to be quarantined."

"Exactly," confirms Ruby. "On the surface it looks like they're trying to screen for Balinson's disease."

"I thought that had been eradicated," says Raj.

"Most places," says Ruby. "Not everyone in the Belt has access to the vaccines, though."

Lasadi nods slowly. "So a special medcheck request for Balinson's could be completely legitimate, given how far out in the Belt the *Slingshot* runs?"

Ruby smiles tightly. "It could have been, exactly. But the code's actually a flea that lets the owner get deeper access if they want."

"Targeted at us?"

"Doesn't seem so. Looks like a standard part of the *Slingshot*'s handshake. It sat dormant in our system until after dinner tonight. There's more." Ruby swipes a set of messages onto her tablet. "I got into that private data cube Alex cloned in Escat's office and found a backup of his correspondence that's been wiped from the system."

She glances at Raj; he continues. "Escat exchanged messages with Karl Gatmaitan a few weeks back, trying to set up a meeting about some new technology Gatmaitan had developed."

"Vash and Gracie said they were talking about going into business together," Lasadi says.

"Escat was, at least." Raj looks grim. "Gatmaitan told him no, and two days later, he was dead. I told Escat no this afternoon, and tonight someone tried to kill us. It would have looked like an accident, too."

"We don't know he killed Gatmaitan."

"Don't we?" Jay asks. He's not sitting at the table with the rest of them, he's been leaning against the counter with arms crossed over his chest, dark brows pulled together and a storm in his eye. She hasn't asked why he'd still been up working while the rest of them were getting ready for bed; she's found him in the engine room at all hours, especially when he's upset and hasn't found the words to talk about it. It has something to do with her, she knows, but she's grateful now she hadn't addressed the tension she felt at dinner. If she had, and Jay'd gone straight to bed, they might all be dead.

Now he's watching her with a firm steadiness that should reassure her, but instead disquiets her.

"We know someone killed Gatmaitan," he says. "Why not Escat?"

"We don't know anyone killed him," Lasadi says. "You're speculating."

"It might not be Escat," Ruby says before Jay can answer; she shoots him a warning glance and Lasadi gets the sudden impression the two of them have been discussing this over for the last few hours. "But if someone's killing people who come in with flash tech, we absolutely lit up a neon sign about ours."

Lasadi rolls her shoulder to ease the pinched nerve, tamping down her frustration.

"It tracks," she admits. Jay's not wrong, but he's pulling them off focus. "So we move up the timeline. We already have everything we need to break into the director's unit and steal those notes for Vash and Gracie. We take care of that tonight, then disappear."

Jay's shaking his head. "We can't just leave. If people are being murdered, we have an obligation to help."

"And we have an obligation to find the bastard who did this." Ruby squeezes her brother's arm. "I'd love a few minutes alone with him."

"And we owe it to Gracie and Vash to find out what

happened to their friend," says Alex, shaking off his sister's touch with annoyance. "Right?"

A headache is building in Lasadi's left temple; she turns to Raj, who's been watching them all in silence, and raises an eyebrow. "Thoughts?"

"I can guarantee Gracie and Vash wouldn't want us to put ourselves in danger," he says, and relief trickles through her. "In fact, if they knew what had happened they'd tell us to get the hell out now without bothering with the notes."

"Thank the olds someone else here sees reason." Lasadi pushes herself away from the table. She needs to move, needs sleep, needs to get away from this place where someone tried to hack her ship and kill her crew. She won't feel comfortable until the *Slingshot* is another speck in the black. "Job's still on, but we'll move up the timeline and get out of here ASAP."

"Las." Raj's voice is soft but firm. "When I said Gracie and Vash wouldn't want us to put ourselves in danger, I wasn't suggesting we leave. I want to shut this bastard down before he kills anyone else, and make sure the whole world knows he's a murderer."

Lasadi stills, stomach sinking as she realizes what he's saying. They all want to stay.

"I can't accept the risk," she says.

Jay's nostrils flare. "Is this a double standard, then?"

Lasadi turns to him, confused. "What are you talking about?"

"We go all the way to Sapis to save Kitty the rich party girl — no offense, Ruby — but we won't lift a finger to help working-class folks being preyed on?"

"That is *not* what we are doing."

"Then what? Locking ourselves away in the *Nanshe*?"

"I am trying to keep this crew *safe*."

"You're hiding, Las."

"What the fuck are you — "

"Enough! Saints!" Ruby throws up her hands. "We all need some sleep, don't we. Jay and I did a flash job on the system, so we can shut our eyes without worrying someone's going to mess with us again. And we'll decide what to do in the morning — that's as soon as we can move the timeline up anyway. Even if we weren't all exhausted, Alex is in no shape to go thieving right now."

"I feel fine."

"You'll feel fine when I say you do," Ruby snaps at him, then sighs. "See, we're all bothered up right now." Ruby fixes Lasadi with a stare, then Jay. "You two work it out. I'm not waking up with you glowering at each other."

Ruby's out of line, and Lasadi's about to shut her down when she catches a glimpse of Jay's face. The corner of his mouth has tugged into a smile.

"Yes, Mom," he says wryly, and the barb of tension between them that's been setting Lasadi's every nerve on fire ebbs as he turns that rueful smile on her. Olds. She's exhausted. And she's wound up — Ruby's right, they all are. Lasadi finds herself smiling back at Jay, then turns to give Ruby a salute.

"Understood, Admiral."

"You can both fuck off." Ruby says it with an eye roll, but her shoulders have relaxed, too. "You know I'm right."

"Everybody get some sleep," Lasadi says. "We'll figure out a plan in the morning."

"Good," says Ruby, pushing herself to her feet. "No more emergencies tonight, I mean it. A girl needs her rest."

"I promise, no more emergencies." Lasadi turns to Jay. "I'm sorry. I'm on edge." And if she's honest, she's not used to Jay pressing his own plan so fiercely. "You're not wrong."

"And I understand your worry," Jay says. "But this is important, Las."

It may be four against one in favor of staying, but Lasadi could still overrule them if she wanted to. If this was Jay and a clutch of Garnet mercs, she would — but with this crew she's the captain, not their dictator. And keeping that role with integrity means listening.

"We'll look into it," Lasadi promises. "In the morning."

Jay pulls her into a hug. "We're okay, Las," he murmurs. "And none of us is going anywhere."

Lasadi's breath catches; she's been trying to push the image of her dead crew out of her head for the last few hours, and even though Jay's comment is meant to reassure, it's put more fractures in the fragile shell she's been cobbling together around her fear.

"Thanks to you."

"Any time," he says with a wink, releasing her. "G'night."

As the others drift into their rooms, Lasadi finds herself lingering in the galley, that wild rush of worry she's been keeping at bay slipping back in and squeezing like a hand around her heart. She lets it ebb — it's getting easier lately, she notes. This little crew has made managing that crushing pressure both easier and harder all at once.

Because Jay is right. She's let her world expand beyond the two of them to include this tiny crew, and she's not sure she wants the responsibility of any more souls on her conscience. Jay, on the other hand, would take on any stray they came across. And Lasadi can't keep them locked away safely on the *Nanshe* forever.

"Lasadi."

She turns at Raj's voice.

"You okay?"

She toys with a dozen answers before deciding to go with the truth. "No."

The word takes some of her heaviness with it, and Lasadi stretches out her hand, takes his, tugs him closer until the length of his body has drifted to press against hers. His fingers smooth over her jaw, cup the back of her neck. Lasadi melts into the kiss. She hasn't been able to shake the image of his eyelashes fluttering, breath stilling on his lips, the knowledge it could have been the last thing she ever saw. But the heat of his body and fire of his kiss are doing a damned good job of burning away that shadow.

"Grab that privacy shield?" Lasadi murmurs into Raj's ear.

The vibration of his reply against her collarbone thrums through her core. "Absolutely, Captain."

CHAPTER 17
JAY

YES, I'M FREE. SAME BAR? TEN MINUTES.

It's been five minutes since Jay got that message, but Malcolm's already sitting at the bar in the aft end of Module E where they'd shared a beer after the mystix game. Today he's wearing a gray jumpsuit unbuttoned and tied at the waist to reveal a simple black T-shirt. Something about this worker's outfit rather than the nicer clothes he was wearing yesterday makes him look younger.

Or maybe it makes him look his true age. Jay would guess Malcolm's little older than twenty, the same age he'd been when he first left his father's union and went to join the CLA. An age where you feel invincible, where the whole world stands before you for the taking.

Jay tips a nod at the bartender, who, after a glance at Malcolm, returns it with a friendly greeting. Last time Jay walked into this bar he'd been a stranger; this time he's clearly with Malcolm. Whoever Malcolm is on this ship, it apparently counts for something with the workers — a good sign. That's one lesson Jay learned working for Nico Garnet: You can tell a lot about someone's character from how the staff treat them in the places where they're regulars.

"'The Flicks,'" Malcolm says when Jay walks over to his table, reading Jay's shirt.

"Kafusa band from Corusca. You heard of them?"

"I haven't."

"They're wild. I saw them in person when I was a kid — really good show. I'll send you a playlist."

"I'd like that. They probably won't get out to perform on the *Slingshot* anytime soon."

"Doubt it."

"Maybe we'll have to start a band of our own out here. You play anything?"

"Air drums," Jay says; Malcolm laughs, hazel eyes sparkling. "Beer? I think I owe you this time."

"Not here." Malcolm stands, shares a glance with the bartender. "Come on. Your message said you wanted to learn more about life in the black, right? Let me show you something."

Malcolm doesn't head out the way Jay came in — back towards the *Nanshe*'s midclass berth. Instead they leave through the aft entrance of Module E, which opens into an identical module. There are five of these docking modules trailing off the *Slingshot*'s marketplace, Jay remembers, and the *Nanshe* is docked with the closest.

The pricing goes down the further a berth is from the marketplace, and it's clear the quality of the accommodations does, too. The community services hubs and facilities Jay and Malcolm pass are even more dingy than the ones in the *Nanshe*'s module, with Out of Service signs on half the doors and vending machines standing mostly empty. Meaning if you want to restock or shower, you have to head to the more expensive modules anyway.

"We're in the true heart of the ship," Malcolm says as they enter what should be the final services hub. By Jay's count, there's one docking module left before the aft propulsion unit. "The true heart of the Belt."

"Folks in the Pearls tell me they're the heart of the Belt."

"Of course they do." Malcolm laughs. "The Belt's full of bubbles, families drifting alone in mining claims or ships. And the stations — Lan Se, Maribi, Xichin — they're bigger versions of the same bubbles. The Pearls are another bubble, as isolated as the stations. But here on the *Slingshot*, everyone mixes together."

To Jay, this section of the *Slingshot* feels more like home than the rest of the ship. There are more families docked at these cheaper berths — with more mouths to feed, you can't splurge on accommodations. Kids play in the lounge areas, grandparents sit and chat, small clans and individuals all enjoying the ride together. The facilities may be out of service, but there's more laughter here. More sharing of what little resources they do have, like Jay's own family had. Even when there wasn't much money, there'd always been enough food on the table for friends who had even less. No one ever complained, they just pulled up another chair and divvied the portions into six instead of five.

Malcolm is studying Jay as he takes in the scene. "These are the people that keep the Belt alive," he says with satisfaction. He turns to a middle-aged woman in a faded and frayed black jumpsuit. Two fingers on her right hand are missing, which is oddly comfortable to Jay, too. Plenty of the people in his father's union were missing fingers. "Did you get that new recycler unit, Marie?"

"Saint," the woman says, grinning. Jay can't tell if it's a greeting; she doesn't seem to be using the word as a curse like Ruby does. "I did, thank you."

Malcolm tips her a nod. "Of course."

Jay trails Malcolm as he makes the rounds. There's a certain weight to how people greet him in this module, a certain deference despite his youth. Jay, on the other hand, is getting curious looks. He suspects if he wasn't here with Malcolm the reception would be chillier. Not outright cold, but suspicious — and rightly so. These people will take care of their own, but they don't yet know if Jay is one of their own, or a predator. But no one will question Malcolm for bringing him here.

So. Who in the names of the old ones is Malcolm?

Yesterday, Jay had gotten the sense Malcolm was socially connected. He figured Malcolm could give him some insight on what the social strata of the *Slingshot* was like — and what he'd meant when he said Escat was playing with fire. He'd also likely be a good candidate to help them spread news of whatever evidence Raj and Ruby could find on Director Escat, if they determined he was the one behind the attack.

Malcolm had said he was here to look out for people on the *Slingshot*, and from what Jay can see, that tracks. Despite his youth, he has a similar energy to Jay's father, the man who knew everyone in the neighborhood by name and couldn't walk ten meters without running into someone to talk to. Much to a young Jay's chagrin.

At a lull in the activity, Malcolm turns back to Jay. "What made you join the CLA?"

Jay nods at the kid Malcolm had been talking to, a young girl traveling with her older cousins. "Her."

"Altha?" Malcolm smiles. "Awfully specific."

"Kids like her back on Corusca," Jay says. "My folks tried to make a good life for my sisters and I. We didn't have much, but we were comfortable — and I could see how much harder it was going to be for families like ours if Corusca joined the Alliance. My dad fought in his own way, with his union. But I felt like I should do something more."

"And you decided to take up arms."

"Guess so."

"If the Alliance ever comes sniffing around the Belt, we'll need people like you."

"We're a long way from that," Jay says, but he's having trouble brushing the thought off. He's always thought of Corusca as the last non-Alliance stronghold to fall. After all, Arquelle had already strong-armed the rest of the countries on Indira into joining; it was no surprise they'd turned to Indira's moon to complete their hand.

But maybe their ambitions of empire are hungrier than can be contained by the gravitational pull of Indira. Maybe the rest of the Durga System saw Corusca's stand not as the Alliance's final conquest, but as the final line of defense before the Alliance started expanding their grasp beyond Indira and its moons.

Does the Alliance really have their sights on New Sarjun? On the Pearls? All the way out to Bixia Yuanjin? Maybe they do. After all, Jay saw an Alliance cargo ship near the Pearls a few days ago with his own eyes.

Jay'd always figured they lost the war, but maybe the fight for Corusca was just a battle. Look at New Manila, where the New Manila Liberation Front is constantly gathering strength and testing the Alliance's presence within their borders. Or the Teguçan insurgent attacks that caused the Alliance to pull troops from there last year. It might have lasted only a few months before the Alliance returned with even more brutal force, but the Teguçan rebels had won a victory.

Still.

"I can't see the Alliance trying to control the entire Belt," Jay says.

"I'd like to see them try. They might win the Pearls, but the rest of us will slip through their fingers like dust and fight back."

That might be true. There are hundreds of private compounds scattered through the belt, like Rasheda

Auburn's abandoned station or the Traveler's Emporium, and there are dozens of public stations like Lan Se, Maribi, and Xichin. They're all part of the Federation, technically, but like the hubs in Ironfall, each has its own informal structure of government: collective, cartel, committee, or even crime organization similar to the Garnets'. The difference is the hubs of Ironfall are each a short tram ride away from one another. They share the same rock, the same resources. If push came to shove, they'd *have* to work together. The scattered Belt stations are days and weeks apart, with nothing but human kindness to incentivize them to band together.

Maybe that will be their strength when the Alliance comes knocking. Or maybe it'll be their downfall.

"What would the rest of the Belt be without the Pearls, though?" Jay lifts his hands. "I don't mean it as offense — I'm an outsider. You said yourself the people on the *Slingshot* are the heart of the Belt, but they're only here because they're traveling between their claims and the Pearls."

"The Pearls is *our* Alliance," Malcolm says. "Without the Federation, other stations could become equally powerful. Even the *Slingshot* — which our people rely on — belongs to them. They say it's run as a public service, but look at Escat, lining his own pockets with our blood and sweat."

It's as good an opening as any.

"You said something yesterday," Jay says. "That Escat was playing with fire. What did you mean?"

Malcolm gives him a sly smile. "And *you've* been asking about Karl Gatmaitan."

Jay doesn't bother asking how Malcolm knows; the bartender told him, or one of the players at the mystix table, or both. Malcolm wants Jay to know he has friends everywhere, and that he asked around about Jay to vet him before welcoming him deeper into his world.

Whatever the test was, Jay must have passed it.

Jay debates coming up with a story for Malcolm about why he's so interested in Gatmaitan, but people like this don't respect stories. They respect the truth.

"Friend of a friend," Jay says. "They didn't like the line they were fed about a heart attack, asked me to look into it."

"Escat's getting sloppy."

"So this isn't his first time?"

"There have been a half-dozen other strange deaths on the *Slingshot* over the past few years. Every single one of them an accident." Malcolm lifts an eyebrow. "Yet every single one lined Escat's pocket."

"Interesting coincidence. You have proof?"

A slow smile spreads across Malcolm's face. "Absolutely."

CHAPTER 18
RAJ

"Are your magboots not working?"

Raj frowns over his shoulder at Ruby, tests the catch. Heels click into place on the metal corridor — nothing's wrong.

"They're fine. Why?"

"Because your head's brushing the ceiling with every step, loverboy."

Raj can't help the smile that flashes across his face. "Don't know what you're talking about."

She's right; he's floating this morning. He woke up tangled in bed with Lasadi Cazinho, which makes him the luckiest man in the system. Some last piece of the ice wall that's been keeping her at arm's length melted through last night, and this morning every inch of his body is blazing with Lasadi's sudden, glorious fire. His soul is blazing, too — she's shown him tantalizing glimpses of her true self before, in those rare moments when she let her guard down. But last night she dropped the shield completely. Like she finally admitted to herself how much she cared for them all, no matter how much potential pain that opened her up to.

How can he convince her that letting herself love this crew won't cause her to lose them like she did Mercury Squadron? How can he show her that the fire of her passion and fury is every bit as powerful as the stone-cold badassery of her self-control?

Because Lasadi'd had ice water coursing through her veins when she bluffed Anton in New Manila, when she unmasked her abuser as a traitor and delivered him to the NMLF. It was one of the sexiest things Raj had ever seen — or, it was once he was free of his shackles and had realized he wasn't about to face an NMLF firing squad.

If she can learn to tap into the full range of her strength she'll be unstoppable.

Raj hadn't been able to tear his eyes off her this morning, and he absolutely does not care who knows it. Even the fact that they're most certainly about to face the man who tried to kill them can't tarnish his mood.

Of course, sooner or later she'll realize the number one threat to her crew is harboring an Alliance fugitive. Eventually she'll come to her senses and send him on his way — but Raj will hold on to this giddy feeling as long as he can, no matter how selfish he knows he's being.

Ruby nudges him from behind before they reach the entrance to the first-class lounge.

"What?"

"I *said*, did you double-check the samples." Ruby arches an eyebrow. "I need your brain in your head, love. This man tried to kill my brother."

"We'll get him for that, and of course I checked the samples." Raj pats the bag over his shoulder, then gives Ruby a once-over. "That's your idea of what an inventor wears, is it?"

"It's what Virginie Walter, Inventor Extraordinaire wears." Ruby winks and gives a little spin. She's pulled her wavy black hair into a messy bun on the top of her head and is wearing a flight suit zipped up more modestly than usual to cover the gold tattoos of the Pearls on her collarbones. It's topped with a teal cardigan that somehow manages to be both frumpy and stylish. She's foregone her usual carmine-red lipstick for a frosty pink that looks garish with her dark skin, and added a slash of bright blue to her lash line. Chunky bracelets adorn both wrists.

At a second look, she *does* look like a recluse who dug through her closet for forgotten makeup and her nicest sweater for an important meeting.

Inventor Extraordinaire Virginie Walter is a new addition to the con, cooked up this morning as they pivoted their plan over vast amounts of coffee. The original ruse was meant merely to get Alex access to Escat's office, not to stand up under scrutiny. Not that Ruby's cobbled-up namidium-finding tech won't pass a few basic demonstration tests, but if they want to get evidence from Escat without tipping him off, they'll need to drown him in science razzle-dazzle. When Raj's sleep-deprived brain was having trouble memorizing chemistry jargon, Ruby finally threw up her hands and insisted on coming with.

Raj palms the entry pad to the first-class lounge and it lights up with his current alias — Ian Chaulet — and a note that reads, WELCOME, GUEST! Beside him, Ruby's posture shifts. Her natural grace melts away as she locks her magboots to the floor, projecting a distracted, nervous energy and taking everything in with wide eyes.

"You're scary good at getting in character," Raj murmurs.

"I'll leave the scary for the bastard who hacked our ship," Ruby whispers back.

"You'll be good, yeah?" Raj is nearly certain Director Daniel Escat is behind last night's attack on the *Nanshe*, but he also knows what a dangerous place "nearly certain" is to be. Decide one thing is true too early, and it blinds you to the subtle details and options you wouldn't see otherwise.

"I'll be nice. I've wanted to murder my brother plenty of times, haven't I. I get it." Raj shoots her a look and she waves a hand. "You don't have to worry about me. Let's get this bastard."

The first-class lounge is done up in showy finery, with gold-plated tabletops and shimmering biosilk curtains framing the portholes. There are a dozen tables scattered tastefully around the lounge, and five private booths lining one wall, each with half-circle benches of brilliant blue faux leather so fine it could pass as the real thing, and isolation shields so the occupants can conduct business without being overheard.

Who this show is directed at, Raj couldn't say. The *Slingshot*'s first-class berths seem to be rarely filled, and this morning, only one of the booths is being used by guests. Two figures cast shadows against the isolation shield, leaning forward over their breakfasts. Director Escat has been waiting for them in a second booth. He stands when they enter.

"Good morning!" He holds out a hand to Raj, then Ruby, his wide, politician's smile beaming on them both. "Thank you for meeting me here. It's so much more comfortable than my office."

The last-minute change of venue had been a surprise, but Raj isn't yet sure what it means. It could be Escat realized his office was bugged and that Alex had rifled through his desk — but the kid is so subtle even Raj had nearly missed it. It could be that Escat's worried they suspect him for their ship's malfunction last night and wants witnesses in case they try to attack him.

And if Escat *hadn't* tried to kill them last night — Raj has promised Lasadi he'll keep an open mind — it could just mean he's showing off the luxury he has access to. Morning coffee in a fancy first-class lounge isn't a bad opening gambit when it comes to wooing a business partner.

Work with me and this, too, can be yours.

Escat ushers them to one of the private booths, which are each set in their own glass bubble. Up close it's clear each bubble features a full, unblocked view of the starry expanse outside the *Slingshot*. Raj's eyes widen — it's stunning. But it's definitely not going to work for this meeting.

"Gorgeous, isn't it," Ruby says, her voice a touch more breathy than it should be for Inventor Extraordinaire Virginie Walker, smile a touch too bright. He can see her pulse fluttering in the hollow of her throat. "Lovely."

"It is," Raj agrees. "Scary as hell though, right?" He laughs and slides a finger down the transparency panel until the glass turns a translucent, milky blue, leaving a narrow sliver of a window at eye level. Ruby shoots him a grateful look, then joins him in the booth.

"Glad you could meet us," Raj says as Escat takes his seat. "Let me introduce Virginie Walter. She's the brains behind this contraption — I'm just the shill. I figure you'll have questions she can answer better."

"A pleasure," Escat says. "I trust you enjoyed your first night on the *Slingshot*."

Escat's tone is perfectly polite, but his smile seems plastered on; there's a sheen of sweat on his brow despite the pleasant temperature in the lounge.

"We had a bit of an adventure, actually." Raj leans in, like *Have I got a story for you*. "Something went wrong with our atmosphere mixture, coulda poisoned us all! Lucky we've got Ginnie here, she caught it before it got too far." Raj shakes his head with a bemused grin. "Space, man. Always trying to kill you."

"Oh?" Escat's voice comes out hoarse. He clears his throat, surreptitiously wipes away a bead of sweat. "That's terrible. If you'd like, I could have one of the ship's mechanics come by to look at your system."

"All good." Raj waves away Escat's concern. If he'd had any doubts before this meeting that the director was behind the attempt on their lives, they're gone now. And he's sure as hell not going to invite one of Escat's lackeys onto the *Nanshe* to finish the job. "Probably happens all the time — but we're not here to talk about our janky ship systems! Ginnie, show him."

Ruby's eyes light up as she pulls the device out of her shoulder bag and sets it on the table. "Ian said he already demonstrated what the detector can do, but let me explain *how*. This is my favorite part."

Raj has heard her go through the technical details of the device a dozen times before, mostly while she was trying to teach him to give this spiel himself, so he tunes her out and focuses on watching Escat. The director seems to be shaking off his nerves; he probably thought Raj was about to accuse him of tampering with their ship, but since the subject was raised and ignored, Escat is starting to relax. Bastard thinks he got away with it.

Now he's leaning forward as Ruby rambles on about the science behind her discovery — which makes him either a decent actor or a complete sociopath.

Though, Raj supposes, Escat doesn't have to be either. He's a politician, and Raj has known plenty of those in his life. As an admiral in the Arquellian navy, his father'd had a peer group filled with social movers, career politicians, and the upper crust of Arquellian society — and all their vicious social games. Raj doesn't think any of them explicitly tried to kill each other, but they certainly did their share of political backstabbing throughout the years.

And who knows. Maybe murder *was* on the table. After all, Raj's father hadn't hesitated to order his own son's death. Raj won't put anything past Escat.

"Yes, I see." Escat finally waves a hand as Ruby heads off on a tangent describing the paper she read a few years back that posits the existence of trace molecular disturbances in the growth of crystal patterns in asteroids as related to the presence of lead. Raj hasn't been following her act at all, but knowing Ruby, she actually did read the paper and the anecdote is going somewhere. She trails off as Escat leans forward.

"Who else have you told about this?" Escat asks.

Ruby draws her brows together. "The paper is publicly published," she says. "When you look at these crystals under shortwave UV, they — "

"Who have you told about your *own* discovery," Escat says impatiently. He points to the vial of sample rock.

"Oh!" Ruby shrugs and looks at Raj. "I don't talk to a lot of people."

"We're debuting it here," Raj says smoothly. "The passengers of the *Slingshot* are getting the first chance at it."

"Yes, yes. And you had your little demonstration yesterday in the marketplace. But who else have you *met with*?"

Raj lifts an eyebrow. "Only you."

"Glad to hear it." Escat sits back and scrubs the palms of his hands down his thighs. "Because I have a proposition for you."

Raj keeps his expression casual like a good businessperson should, though he allows a glimmer of anticipation through for Escat's benefit. Ruby shoots Raj an excited look; Virginie Walter, Inventor Extraordinaire wouldn't be skilled at bluffing during business negotiations.

"You obviously have a sound product," Escat says. "But doing presentations one at a time is inefficient, is it not? I can see Ms. Walter's brilliant mind is wasted having conversations like this rather than spending more time in her lab. Wouldn't it make more sense to license the device once and sell it thousands of times without lifting a finger yourself?"

Raj frowns at him. "You're talking about going into business together?"

"I'm talking about buying the sole license to use your product. People will come to me to test their samples, rather than shipping them back to an expensive lab in Artemis City. I pay you a fee per use, which means you get money without the hassle of the hustle, and the technology isn't out there in the world where anyone could replicate it and cut you out."

"I don't know if — "

"At least look at my offer," Escat says. "I took the liberty of drawing up an offer based on similar arrangements I've made in the past. Think of it as an opening bid."

He flicks a document off his comm and onto the table in front of them, Raj skims through it as though reading the clauses, but in reality his mind is racing.

Is Escat changing tactics, now that he knows Ruby locked him out of the *Nanshe*'s system? If he can't kill them and make it look like an accident, in order to steal their tech outright, he might be trying to trap them into a contract. There are nerves under Escat's faux-friendly smile, an urgency in the way he's watching them study the offer. Escat *needs* this opportunity. The levelheaded investor with his bevy of mines and Federation salary is looking for a new windfall, and judging by the insistent messages he'd been sending Gatmaitan before the inventor died, he needs it fast.

Why does he need the new income so badly?

The vendor Lasadi had spoken with, Fiona, she'd said Escat had dangerous new friends. The man Jay had met, Malcolm, he'd said Escat was playing with fire.

Escat's under pressure from somewhere, and he's willing to kill for a windfall that will get him out of it.

Raj sticks out his hand. "Director Escat, I think we can come up with a way to work together. We'll take a closer look at this offer and get back to you by the end of the day."

Escat's hand is clammy. "Don't dally," he says. "The sooner we can get started, the better for everyone."

"I agree."

"One more thing," Escat says. "No one's spoken to *you* about this, have they?"

Raj shares a curious look with Ruby; she shrugs. "No," he says.

"Good, good. Let's keep this under wraps until we announce this partnership together."

Raj gives Escat his brightest smile. "Absolutely. We'll be in touch."

Ruby drops her wide-eyed inventor's facade once they've left the lounge, a mask of fury slipping into its place.

"I could kill that rat bastard with my bare hands," she snarls.

"I still need to know why he did it," Raj says. "It's not just greed — he's got trouble on his heels."

"I frankly don't give a shit about the *why*, love. I want to see him out an airlock."

"Creditors?" Raj cracks his neck, ignoring her. "He could easily be living beyond his means out here."

Ruby shoots him a dark look.

"Or his bosses have finally noticed what he's up to and are starting to ask uncomfortable questions." Raj shakes his head. "I don't see how a new namidium windfall would help in that case, unless he's hoping to bribe his way out. I don't think that usually works with the Federation."

"So he's planning to pull up his stakes and run," Ruby says. "Which means if I'm going to watch him suffocate to death we need to make it fast."

"Running doesn't track," says Raj. "Where'll he run to?

Bixia Yuanjin? His wealth is tied up in his Belt mining operations, and those would be tough to manage from anywhere but the Pearls. If he were planning on leaving Federation space, he wouldn't be investing in us. No. Escat's betting on staying here, and this is his way of doubling down."

Ruby's smile could cut diamonds. "Let him try."

CHAPTER 19
LASADI

THE ENERGY OF THE CROWD PRESSES AGAINST LASADI LIKE A physical force when she enters the marketplace. It's more packed than yesterday, louder, with passengers congregating on the platforms in a crush of bodies and conversation. Yet despite the gathered crowd, quite a few more vendor stalls are shuttered. She checks the time — about midmorning, locally. Some sort of holiday? Or maybe vendors normally don't open until afternoon.

Lasadi scans the crowd, a worry gnawing at her that almost makes her nostalgic for the bad old days when she was working for Nico Garnet. She hadn't enjoyed much about those years, where even the most delicious meal had tasted like rusted iron, but Nico's jobs had kept her alive, paid off her debt, and — most importantly — hadn't mattered one bit.

Every time they left Ironfall, Lasadi had one objective: make sure Jay got home all right. Whether or not they achieved what Nico had asked them to do was secondary — she could sweet-talk Nico if they failed. If she were killed it would hardly matter, because she was dead anyway. On the rare times Nico had sent mercs with her, it would have damaged her professional pride for one of them to die, but she wouldn't have mourned them. She'd barely learned their names.

Since taking on a permanent crew, she's expanded her definition of success from "Jay survives" to "we all survive," herself included. But this? Watching a crowd of unfamiliar faces and knowing some unseen danger stalks them, and she could do something about it? She's not sure she's ready to have the fates of strangers on her shoulders again.

Her readiness doesn't matter, though. Because Jay is. Raj, Ruby, Alex — they all are. Which means Lasadi needs to learn how to be ready, too.

"Heya," says a voice at her shoulder; Lasadi turns to find the woman with the shaved head and scalp tattoos she'd talked to yesterday. She's wearing the same yellow jumpsuit as yesterday, with a bright blue flash of undershirt peeking out from the zipper.

"Oh, hey. Fiona, right?"

"Yeah. And you were M.J.?"

"Good memory." And good thing, too. Lasadi had been racking her own brain to remember what alias she'd picked out of thin air yesterday when they last spoke. She glances up at the crowd. "Quite the turnout today. Is it normally this busy?"

Fiona shrugs. "Depends on where we are in the run. We're still pretty close to the Pearls, so it's as full as the *Slingshot* ever gets — once we're really out in the black we can go days without picking up new passengers, and the ones we do pick up are normally broke and exhausted. Though there's always one or two who got a payday. It makes the energy weird. That's why I prefer the trip out — everyone's mostly excited."

"People definitely seem excited today."

Fiona makes a noncommittal noise. "You're not from around here, right?"

"No. Corusca."

A smile lights up Fiona's face. "Really? I wondered." Her gaze flicks to Lasadi's stud earrings. "You're wearing Coruscan opal, it's got those unique flecks of red in it. You don't see it out here much."

"You know your stones."

"I spend most of my days talking to belt miners. Before long, the conversation always goes to pretty rocks or survival gear." Fiona laughs. "Or the best ways to distill liquor, obviously."

"Gotta pass the time," says Lasadi.

"Exactly. But let me give you a tip. Someone offers you a cut from their still, take a look at their teeth first. If they're pitted, it's probably laced with seraph."

"Another good way to pass the time, I suppose." The combination of stimulant and epic hallucinations is what makes seraph such a popular party drug back in Artemis City, but you can always tell the ones who've gotten too hooked. They tend to flare bright, burn out fast. And it wreaks havoc on your tooth enamel.

"I've never tried. Got too much to live for." Fiona tilts her head to study Lasadi. "Doesn't look like you need to brew your own spirits, anyway."

"I'm doing all right for now." Lasadi needs to turn the conversation from whether or not she can afford to buy spirits instead of bootleg them; she's not sure how to answer if Fiona starts prying into what she does. "You been here long? On the *Slingshot*?"

"Better part of the year," Fiona says. "Things were getting a bit crowded at home with my younger siblings, so it was time to make something of myself."

"I had a younger brother and sister at home," says Lasadi

before she can stop herself. "Have," she corrects. "Though they're not really at home anymore. My brother got married — he's got a kid now. And my sister . . ." Deserves a reply Lasadi doesn't know how to formulate. "Yeah, I was definitely ready to leave home once the time came."

"It was either leave to start my own trade or stay and play mother to the youngest ones, and I knew I'd be tearing my hair out and slipping seraph into the homebrew like the rest of them if I stuck around." Fiona shrugs. "This isn't what I dreamed I'd do when I was a little girl, but at least I'm working for myself. Nothing beats that."

"Agreed. It can be lonely, though."

"Doesn't have to be," says Fiona. "Belt's full of drifters, but that doesn't mean we don't care for each other. There's a special sort of community out here. You just have to scratch the surface a little harder to find it." She gives Lasadi a smile, edged with worry. "It was nice chatting. I get tired of conversations with miners — you can only talk ore for so long without losing your mind. Let's grab a drink after all this if you have time."

Lasadi frowns at her. "After all what?"

"The protest," Fiona says, lifting her chin to the gathering crowd. As they've been talking, the marketplace has gotten even more crowded, and now Lasadi is looking for it she can tell something about the energy is off from yesterday. The friendly social buzz has shifted into something more aggressive; what few stalls were still open when she entered are closing down now.

Fiona studies the crowd a moment, expression drawn. "I'm gonna check my stall. It's going to get pretty stormy in here in a few minutes."

"What are people protesting?"

"Didn't you hear? Director Escat has been accused of murder."

Lasadi doesn't bother hiding her surprise, though it's

not at Fiona's revelation. How the hell did word get out already? Were Raj and Jay so certain of Escat's involvement they decided to spark rumors without checking back in? No, impossible. There must be another explanation.

Either way, their timeline has shortened, and Lasadi needs to get to the others.

"I hadn't heard," Lasadi says. "Maybe I'll go check it out."

"Not sure I'd recommend that. These sorts of crowds can get violent."

"I'm sure," Lasadi says. "This sort of thing happen often?"

"More and more," Fiona says darkly.

"What do you mean?"

But Fiona shakes her head like she's shaking away a curse. "None of my business," she says. "Or yours. I'm going to go check on my stall — stay out of trouble."

And she pushes off before Lasadi can ask more.

"Cap." Ruby's come up behind her, trailed by Raj and Alex. She glances after Fiona curiously. "Learn anything interesting from my girlfriend?"

"I learned people are protesting because Escat's been accused of murder, and that she's scared of something but won't tell me what." Lasadi drums her fingertips against her thigh, combing through the rest of her conversation with Fiona for any hint of what could be bothering her. "Please tell me you're not the reason people are protesting."

"Absolutely not," Raj says. "But whoever did is doing us a favor. The asshole looks guilty as hell."

"*Looks* guilty," Lasadi repeats. Olds, but they need hard evidence if they're going to take this man down. "What did you find."

"That he started sweating buckets as soon as he heard about our ship's malfunction, and he's trying to lock us into a quick contract now that he no longer has an easy way to make our deaths look like an accident."

"If the Federation hasn't been able to take him down for confiscating cargo and soliciting bribes, we're going to need harder evidence than buckets of sweat."

Lasadi sighs and turns her face upward. The crowd's energy is crackling above them now, the initial knot of people around the uppermost platforms collecting newcomers like moons, forming a slow drift of untethered bodies. With the mass of humans it's too thick to see the far end of the marketplace, to the door leading towards the first-class portion of the *Slingshot*.

What Lasadi can see, however, is the flicker of a holographic bust on one of the middle platforms. She shifts to get a better look: Karl Gatmaitan. If she listens closely, she can hear his name repeated in the murmur of the crowd.

"We might be able to use this distraction," Lasadi says. "Alex, do you have everything you need to break into the director's unit?"

"Yeah, Cap. Only won't it be more heavily guarded than before?"

"Maybe not. Escat will have to come calm this crowd down eventually. Or at least send his security guards. Ruby, what's the emergency protocol?"

Ruby's red-lacquered fingernails tap the screen of her tablet. She's still wearing her slouchy cardigan and messy bun, the heads-up display perched on her freckled nose casting a blue light on her dark cheeks. "Emergency protocol has the director moving to the forward propulsion unit of the *Slingshot*. There's a secure survival chamber there, and a private shuttle."

"Which, if the security guards are heading here, leaves the director's module practically empty."

"Speaking of," Raj says, gaze shifting past Lasadi.

The *Slingshot*'s security team have started to arrive, and

if Lasadi thought their previous uniforms seemed like riot gear, now they're looking downright deadly. They've still got their electric barbs and batons, but a few now carry pulse carbines. The air around them shimmers with some sort of personal shield. They're not doing anything yet, but their presence isn't helping calm things down, either.

"This was supposed to be a simple job," Lasadi says.

"No such thing," Raj answers lightly. But his flash of a smile is tense. "I'm not opposed to breaking into the director's module right now, but I don't like it. Too many ways this can go wrong, and we still don't have the entire picture."

"Agreed." Lasadi studies the crowd, trying to force the puzzle pieces into place. Whether or not Escat killed Karl Gatmaitan to get his notes, someone besides them wants the world to think he did. "This is the perfect distraction. Except for one thing."

Raj nods. "We didn't create it."

"Right. So who did, and what do they want?" Her comm chimes before any answers click into place, and Lasadi breaths out frustration, swipes open a connection request from Jay.

"Where are you?" she asks.

"Las? Hey, we got a twist."

CHAPTER 20
JAY

JAY'S BEEN KEEPING AN EYE ON THE FOLKS IN THE SERVICES HUB while he and Malcolm talk. While many people are greeting Malcolm like royalty, not everyone's happy he's here. An older woman shoots them both a dirty look after they walk by, hiding it with her drink. A man gathers his two children, making a hurried excuse to his companion as he leaves.

Interesting. Some folks don't like Malcolm, but nobody is willing to show it to his face. It could be because of his position on the Alliance. Even if the locals objectively disagree with the Alliance, it feels like a distant problem — whereas agitators like Malcolm are a very present nuisance. If the Alliance tries to fold the Belt in, Jay suspects many will blame agitators like Malcolm for attracting their attention, rather than blaming the Alliance itself.

Or maybe it's something else. Because when the aft door of the services unit opens and a half-dozen young people float through, the mood instantly sours. The youths are laughing and joking, oblivious to the sudden current of unease that threads through the crowd to brush against the fine hairs on the back of Jay's arms.

"Saint's here!" one of the youths calls, and the rest fall to attention as Malcolm lifts his chin in greeting.

"Is everything ready?" Malcolm asks, and the young man he's addressing nods. Malcolm turns to Jay. "Then it's time. Escat's been drinking blood from the heart of the Belt for too long. The Pearls have been feeding on us for too long. Will you help us take back our birthright?"

Jay holds up his hands. "I'm out of the fighting game. But I appreciate the tour." The shifting atmosphere around Jay isn't subtle. The glitter in Malcolm's gaze intensifies, the body language of his crew becoming more aggressive. No one moves against him, though — might be because they're waiting for Malcolm's signal. "Unless that wasn't an invitation."

"You would know better than anyone that a reluctant fighter hurts the cause," Malcolm says mildly. "I thought you knew we had a mutual enemy."

"What do you mean?"

"Escat tried to kill you and your crew."

Jay stills. "How do you know that?"

"I wish I could say you were the first people Director Escat had tried to attack outright. He's becoming greedy, and I intend to stop him before someone else dies."

"It's not only my decision."

"Then ask your captain," Malcolm says. "But if you'd prefer to go back to your ship and wait out what comes next, we have no bad blood. You and your crew can be on your way. I understand if you'd rather see to your own."

I understand if you'd rather turn tail and save your own ass, Malcolm means, *leaving the rest of us to fend for ourselves. I understand if you've stopped caring about the fate of the working classes. If you're too washed up to still join the fight.*

It's a good play, perfectly calculated based on what Malcolm's gathered so far about Jay — and it might even have worked.

But another thing Jay learned working for Nico Garnet is that you can learn a lot about someone from the way a crowd scatters when their crew enters a room. On his own, Malcolm had been mostly well received. But since his crew showed up in the services hub, the place has quietly become a ghost town.

Something dangerous is brewing, and Jay's not about to let it when he has a chance to head it off. First, though, he needs to figure out what Malcolm's planning.

"My crew aren't cowards," Jay says, and the corner of Malcolm's mouth pulls into a satisfied smile. "We've got your backs."

Jay pulls out his comm, movements slow and easy while Malcolm's crew watch him, heart rate calm and even as he connects the call.

"Where are you?" Lasadi asks. He can hear the sounds of a crowd beneath her voice; she was going to meet the others in the marketplace, and by the hubbub of voices in the background she must be there still.

"Las? Hey, we got a twist."

"You all right? Things are getting tense over here."

"Yeah, I'm all good."

Malcolm's crew are mostly ignoring Jay now, drifting off to make preparations among themselves, but Malcolm himself has stayed close. Jay needs to be very careful how he plays this. If they were having this conversation in person, he could catch Lasadi's eye, let her know what he was really thinking without tipping Malcolm off that Jay is on the fence about him. But they're not. Jay will have to get the message across another way.

"Las, I'm in one of the services hubs out past our berth, with Malcolm. I told you about him? Anyway, he's got an idea he could use our help with, and I think you should hear him out."

"What kind of help?"

"Hold on, I'm putting you on broadcast." Jay glances at Malcolm. "You've got the floor, man."

Malcolm gives him a solemn nod that looks far too serious on his young face. Old ones, but had they all looked so young in the CLA, even as they'd geared up to fight and die with the weight of generations crashing down on their shoulders? They probably had. Only Malcolm and his crew aren't blazing with patriotism and hope — no matter the pretty story he's trying to sell. They're fueled by something entirely different, and Jay needs to find out what it is.

"Captain, my name is Malcolm Saint. It's nice to meet you."

"A pleasure, I'm sure." Lasadi's voice through the comm is formal, guarded.

"I'm not sure what initially brought you and your crew to our piece of space," says Malcolm, "but I think we'll find the timing worked out for both of us. We have a common enemy. Director Escat tried to kill you and your crew, and that's just scratching the surface of his crimes on this ship. We need your help to finish his reign of terror."

Jay can picture Lasadi's expression at the flowery language, her dubious frown. If they were in person, she'd almost certainly be shooting Jay a *Who the hell have you brought me?* look.

That's what Jay's counting on.

"And who do you work for?" Lasadi asks.

"Myself," Malcolm answers. "I call the shots here." It's a touch too defensive, his chest puffed and jaw set. He might call the shots *here*, but he answers to someone, Jay guesses. A local pirate enclave? One of the Ironfall bosses? One of Escat's rivals in the Federation, tired of hearing the rumors and getting no action from their peers, so they've decided to take matters into their own hands?

"You're the ones who spread the rumors that the director is a murderer."

"We're not spreading rumors," Malcolm says. "We're spreading fact."

"Then I assume you have proof? This is a dangerous game to play on a hunch."

The corner of Malcolm's mouth turns up at that. He's one who likes playing dangerous games, Jay thinks. For some people, the chance you might accidentally burn it all to the ground is part of the appeal of playing with fire.

He's probably not working for one of Escat's political rivals, then. If someone was simply out to sabotage Escat's position on this ship, they would have chosen a saboteur less likely to leave a smoking debris field of rubble in his wake.

"Have you hacked into Escat's communications?" Malcolm asks; Lasadi doesn't answer. "If you did, you should be able to see the order he sent to his security chief right before the attack on your ship."

"You're monitoring him?" Lasadi asks; now it's Malcolm who doesn't respond, beyond giving Jay a secret smile. "Hold on."

The atmosphere in the services hub has completely shifted. The families, the locals, everyone who Malcolm had referred to as the "heart of the Belt" had melted out of the way when Malcolm's crew showed up. Now his crew are openly unloading crates filled with weapons and dealing them out.

But to what end?

Sounds like most of the crew are headed towards the marketplace — though Jay can't tell if the plan is to fight the security guards, protect the civilians, or something more sinister. Whatever their goal, the crew moves with alarming efficiency; since Jay started this call the weapons have been passed out, orders have been given, and the services hub is nearly empty once more. A handful of toughs remain with Malcolm and Jay: a petite woman with a long blond braid, a pair of muscle-clad bruisers who look like brothers, a man with a snake tattoo coiled around his throat, and a woman with a badly done eye implant set into a mass of scar tissue. Her cheap prosthetic arm gleams dully in the light.

Jay gives them all a friendly smile; no one returns it.

Fuck, he thinks, because details Malcolm told him earlier are clicking into place. Malcolm had said his parents sent him to live on Maribi Station when he was a teenager, and though he calls himself a protector, no union boss Jay's seen has this much firepower at their disposal. While Malcolm may be young, those under his command obey with a respect that seems rooted in a larger power structure, and while he claims to call the shots here, he reports to someone else.

That, and Jay's seen the shattered-planet tattoo the petite blond woman's sporting before.

Maribi Cartel.

Whatever they're planning, he needs Lasadi to know they can't go along with it.

After a moment, Lasadi's curse sparks through the comms.

"Did you find the message?" Malcolm asks.

"I see it. What do you want from us?"

"It's time for Escat to pay. I can't get to him, he's closed himself off. But he trusts your crew, you've got him wrapped up in your con. I need you to bring him to me."

"And what happens after?"

"Justice is served."

"I'm not going to help you lynch anybody."

Malcolm laughs. "You outsiders all have the same opinion of us. We're not barbarians."

Jay catches Malcolm's eye. "She fought with me," he mouths, and Malcolm nods, his expression growing serious.

"If you fought beside our mutual friend Jay, then you know justice isn't always the default. You know what it is to live under the rule of people who refuse you autonomy and drain your blood to line their own pockets. You know what it is to watch the ones you love die because of the callous actions of a government that doesn't represent you."

Jay breathes a prayer of relief. Thank the old ones, but that is the most perfect thing Malcolm could say to Lasadi right now.

The silence that follows stretches heavy, and Jay can tell Malcolm thinks he's won. It's not a bad assumption. He's making a good play based on what little he knows about Jay and, by extension, Lasadi. He's chosen rhetoric that would probably work on another ex-freedom fighter who still had a bone to pick with the Alliance, and maybe in another life that would have been Jay. But serving under — and being betrayed by — Anton was the perfect vaccine against smooth rhetoric. Jay learned that lesson well enough from the vantage of Anton's outer circle; Lasadi has it seared onto her soul.

"You're right," she finally says. "I do know exactly what that's like. We'll help you."

Malcolm smiles, triumphant. "You have my word justice will be served. Make contact with Escat, keep his trust, and I'll be in touch with more information shortly."

"I'll be waiting. Jay, I'll talk to you soon."

"Sure thing, Las."

Before Jay can slip his comm back into his pocket, Malcolm reaches to cut the connection. Jay tenses; he'd meant to "forget" that step and leave the connection open in hopes the others could continue listening in — does Malcolm suspect him? But Malcolm claps him on the arm, grinning. The gesture was habit, then, not suspicion.

Jay hopes.

"So," Jay says to Malcolm. "We're in. What's next?"

CHAPTER 21
LASADI

JAY'S VOICE CUTS OUT, AND COLD CERTAINTY COILS IN LASADI'S gut. Jay hadn't talked much on the call, but his silence said everything. If he trusted this Malcolm Saint, he would have taken the lead and explained to her why. Instead, he gave Saint the floor and let him strangle himself with his own rhetoric.

Which means Jay's in danger. And Lasadi will tear this ship apart to get him back.

She glances up at the crowd; the mood is getting darker by the moment, and it won't be safe even at the bottom of the marketplace for much longer. They need a plan, and fast.

"Ruby. What have you got for me?"

"The evidence against Escat is there, like Malcolm said it would be. Definitely looks like Escat is the one who accessed the handshake code after sending a message to his security chief about 'pacifying' the crew in our berth. It's keyed to his login alone and encrypted to his biosign."

"There's no way to hack that?"

"I mean, yes. But it would be awfully hard to fake this log, even for me."

"So it's looking like Malcolm Saint's telling the truth. What do you have on him?"

"Looking now, Cap."

"Check to see if there's any record of him visiting Escat," Raj says. "The director seemed like he was getting desperate for an out. If this Saint guy has been putting pressure on him for a while, this might be his way of escalating."

"There's nothing with his name in Escat's calendar."

"Which might mean Escat's keeping those appointments off the books. Remember, he was nervous to meet with someone right after Alex and me. His aide said the person was there waiting, but you couldn't find any evidence of a meeting — in the calendar, or in our surveillance."

Lasadi drums her fingers on her thigh. "Assuming Saint's the one putting pressure on Escat, why keep their meetings secret? And what went wrong?" She lets out a frustrated breath. "We need answers, and it looks like Jay's with the guy who has them. I don't like it, but I think we need to work with Saint until we know what's going on."

"And until we know Jay is safe," says Raj.

Lasadi hadn't wanted to say it out loud because she hadn't wanted to alarm the others, but from their expressions, they've picked up on the gravity of the situation all the same.

"We'll get him back," Lasadi says. "Ruby, I need to know who Saint is, and if he's working on his own. Raj, get with Escat however you can. Alex, you and I are going to have a chat. We still have a heist to plan — only we may be shifting our target."

"We might want to chat somewhere else," Alex says, gaze lifting to the crowd above them. "This neighborhood's starting to go downhill."

Lasadi follows Alex's attention to find a pair floating off

to the side of the crowd. They're both wearing mechanic jumpsuits with no insignia, and though they're not visibly armed, both are carrying duffels that bulge with angular lumps. One leans conspiratorially towards the other; the flash of a metal blade changes hands.

"Good eye."

"I've been learning a lot from my sister's unsavory friends," Alex says grimly. "This is what Ayalasi Kateri was afraid of."

"Well, someone was going to corrupt you." Ruby glances up from her tablet to frown at the suspicious pair, then goes back to her search. "Might as well be us."

"Let's get going," Lasadi says. "Raj, you *can* get back to Escat, can't you?"

"I've got an idea."

"Good. Be careful."

She doesn't stop her hand from drifting his way, doesn't pull back when he catches it, doesn't tense when he brushes a kiss over her knuckles. Ruby's engrossed in her research, Alex is studying the crowd, and neither of them would care even if they did notice the gesture.

It's more than her growing comfort with being affectionate in front of the crew, though. The flecks of gold in Raj's deep brown eyes spark when he smiles, and for once that traitorous voice in her head — *Enjoy that smile now, it'll disappear when you finally show him the real you* — is silent. She's shown Raj *all* her scars, physical and emotional, and, if anything, he seems to want her more.

And it's not just him. Jay, Ruby, Alex, they've all grown closer the more she's been willing to let her guard down. With their help she's clawing her way out of the silent cell she'd fabricated during the Nico Garnet years, and she'll fight tooth and nail anyone who threatens what they're building together now.

"Saints in hell," Ruby groans; she releases her tablet and

pushes her heads-up display to perch daintily on the top of her head.

"What is it?"

"Saint is — oh!" She smiles at someone past Lasadi's shoulder. "Heya."

Lasadi drops Raj's hand and turns to find Fiona approaching; the other woman alights gracefully beside Lasadi, magboots clicking into place. She glances up at the crowd, the tension lines sketched around her eyes and mouth adding a decade to her young face.

"You really should be heading back," Fiona says. "I closed up shop, but things are looking rowdy and I want to keep an eye on the stall in case."

Lasadi shakes her head. "It's going to get ugly. You should come with us."

"I know these people," Fiona says. "I can — " She'd been distracted by the crowd when she approached, but now her gaze shifts past Lasadi to take in the rest of her crew. Her expression grows dark when it lands on Raj. "What the hell are you doing with him?"

Olds, in all her worry for Jay and dread at the stormy crowd gathering overhead, Lasadi had completely forgotten how furious Raj's sales routine had made Fiona yesterday.

"It's not what it looks like," Lasadi says. "I can explain."

"You mean his little show with that miracle technology isn't just another scam?" Fiona gives Raj an arch look. "I can't tell you how many of your kind I've seen come and go, draining people's savings and leaving garbage in your wake." She turns her fury on Lasadi. "And here I thought some outsiders could still be trusted. But apparently you *all* see us as prey."

"It's not like that," Lasadi says, though of course she can't tell Fiona what it *is* like without blowing their cover. "We're here to help."

STAR TRAIN TANGO   173

"Sure you are. Help us out of our money." Fiona's expression shifts when something above them catches her attention. Her brows draw together, teeth catching her lower lip.

Lasadi follows Fiona's gaze; the pair of armed "mechanics" Alex had noticed earlier have been joined by two more. The newcomers aren't bothering to hide their weapons; one has a stun carbine slung over their shoulder, the other is carrying a riot club.

"Who are they?" Lasadi asks Fiona.

"No clue what you're talking about," she says. Her glare still holds anger, but now there's an undercurrent of worry. "I hope I don't see you later."

"Fiona," Lasadi says. "I promise I can explain. You can trust me."

"I can trust you? Bullshit." Fiona glares at her. "You guys are even worse than the cartel. They may be assholes, but they still have to live here with the rest of us — so at least they're assholes who invest in the community so they can leech off it. You all drink our blood and vanish."

Fiona glances once more at the toughs in jumpsuits before pushing past Lasadi and back towards her stall.

Olds be damned, but that went poorly. And this is *exactly* why Lasadi normally lets Jay handle the interactions with outsiders. Maybe he can help her make things up to Fiona after all this is done — and once he's back safe at her side.

Lasadi lets out a deep breath and turns to Ruby. "Cartel?"

"Maribi Cartel," Ruby says. She turns her tablet to the others. "That's what I was about to tell you before my girlfriend showed up. Turns out our new friend Malcolm Saint is a captain in that shitshow, and he's *definitely* the one who met with Escat right after Raj and Alex did."

"If Escat's in bed with the Maribi Cartel, he'd obviously want to keep those meetings secret," Raj says.

"They might not be in bed together," Ruby points out. "They might be strong-arming him."

"Might be both," says Lasadi. "I don't know much about the Maribi Cartel, but I know Nico and Tora avoided them. And that's saying something."

Historically, most of the cargo traveling through the Belt goes through the Pearls. In the past decade, though, more long-haul shippers have started to route themselves through other local stations instead — especially if they're carrying contraband.

Maribi had always been one of the more viable refueling stops, and their customs officials have always been . . . inattentive. The station's influence has grown since the current cartel pushed out the collective government a few years back. All that should have made them excellent business partners for Ironfall bosses like the Garnets, but apparently their viciousness had spooked even ruthless Nico.

"Obvious observation," Alex says. "But we're not on Maribi, only."

"They're making a play for the *Slingshot*," Lasadi says.

"Exactly," says Ruby. "Tying up this market for their drugs and contraband before any of the other groups can. I told you the Belt outside the Pearls was full of pirates and cartels."

Lasadi takes a deep breath. "Well, let's make sure Malcolm can't get hold of the *Slingshot*."

Alex lifts an eyebrow. "So we're helping Escat who tried to murder us? Or we're helping the cartel who's trying to murder him."

If it were up to Lasadi, they'd be doing neither. Instead, she'd be whisking her crew back to the safety of the *Nanshe* to wash their hands of this whole mess — it doesn't need to involve them. But even if Jay was safe and that was an option, it's not the right thing to do.

And she knows exactly what Jay would say if he *was* here. Lasadi glances back up at the crowd, but Fiona has long vanished beyond them.

"We're helping the people caught in the middle," Lasadi says. "Let's get to work."

CHAPTER 22
RAJ

Raj doesn't mind a crowd; crowds in zero G are something entirely different. The three-dimensional crush of bodies, the cacophony of laughter and shouting coming from every direction and bouncing off every hard metal surface in the marketplace — it's next-level chaos.

Still, Raj is reasonably certain they're heading back towards the entrance to the first-class modules and Escat's office. He sticks close to the side of the marketplace, pushing past the shuttered stalls of vendors who, like Fiona, decided to head home early. Sticking close to the wall is the best way to gain purchase and keep from getting stranded in the drifting sea of bodies. Ruby's arm is linked with his as he takes point, and through the babel of the crowd, he hears snatches of her voice apologizing to — or cursing at — the people he shoves past.

The mood of the crowd has gotten uglier since they came through minutes earlier. Previously there'd been a festive atmosphere of curiosity, folks simply drawn together to see what was going on. Now that energy has sparked into a flickering flame, edged with something darker and more dangerous. The makeup of the crowd has changed, too. Where Raj had spotted families twenty minutes ago, those are mostly gone. Anyone not in the mood for violence can surely scent it in the air by now.

It's the perfect environment for someone like Malcolm Saint to pour on an accelerant and have himself a riot.

And Raj would guess that's exactly what's happening, because the shift in mood doesn't seem accidental at all. The agitators Raj spots as he and Ruby push through aren't exactly being subtle.

"Escat will be boarded up, won't he?" Ruby yells from behind him. Raj's shoulder jostles against a teen's back; he and his friends are taking advantage of the chaos to break into a vending machine and steal beers. The teen gives Raj a look of challenge, but Raj just shrugs like *Be my guest.* He's got much bigger things on his mind right now.

"He will," Raj says. "But I'm guessing he'll still be protective of his potential investment — and hopefully the folks who have it in their possession." Raj pushes past another knot of bodies and into blessedly clear space. "If he doesn't have time for a couple of inventors, though, I'm sure he can make time for some federal agents."

"Love it." Ruby squeezes his arm and releases it. "Thank the saints that part's over."

Raj had been worried the throng of protesters would become even denser as they approached the door, but they seem to be concentrated around one of the central platforms where a man is screaming accusations and whipping up dark rhetoric. Here, about fifteen meters from the door, only a few stragglers are listening in. Oh. And about a dozen security guards in full riot gear.

Raj kicks off towards the guards with empty hands held in front of him. A dozen weapons point his way.

"We need to see the director," Raj says as he catches a handhold and comes to a halt a few meters away from the nearest guard. "It's urgent."

"There's a lot of urgent going around right now." The guard points back the way they came. "Head to your bunks. This will calm down soon."

"We can't!" Ruby says, her voice breathy with terror. She clutches her satchel to her chest. "We barely made it as it is! They're trying to steal the device."

The guard frowns at her. "The device?"

"Yes." Ruby glances over her shoulder. "A man with a knife. You have to let us through."

"Call Escat," Raj says. "We met with him earlier today. Ian Chaulet and Virginie Walter, inventors. Well, *she's* the inventor. I'm the one who's going to make the director a rich man, you can ask him yourself." He gives a fast, reflexive grin that fades quickly into worry. "Or send us back into that crowd and lose the director a fortune."

The security guard exchanges shrugs with one of his peers. "Call him."

The other guard turns partly away to make the call; Raj can't hear what he's saying over the ruckus of the crowd, but he can tell the moment their ruse is going to work. The guard's eyes go wide.

"Yes, sir," he says with a glance back at Raj and Ruby. "We'll bring them right in."

The wall of security guards parts for them, as does the door beyond, and Raj and Ruby emerge in a corridor that's every bit as hectic as the marketplace module they just left. The half-dozen security guards on this side are checking weapons and armor; beyond them, passengers are calling out in confusion, trying to figure out what's going on and why the guards won't let them through to the marketplace.

"You!" A guard lifts her stun carbine when she spots Raj, jabbing it at his chest. "No one comes through that door. What are you doing here?"

"The director sent for them," shouts the security guard

who let them through. "Get your asses out here. We need backup." And he vanishes back into the marketplace.

The security guard with the stun carbine slings it over her shoulder, then hooks a thumb behind her. "Then get yourself to his office. I don't have anyone to spare to walk you there."

"That's okay." Raj gives the woman a worried smile. "Be careful out there." He means it. Things are about to get very bad, and the *Slingshot's* security guards probably aren't prepared to do battle with anyone — let alone cartel members who are probably much better armed than the guards expect them to be. Not to mention the ship's passengers, who are being gathered like cannon fodder in the marketplace with no idea of the violence that's ripe to erupt around them.

Escat's aide is waiting for them when Raj and Ruby arrive at the director's module; he shows them into Escat's office without a word, then goes back to gnawing his thumbnail and watching the gathering chaos in the marketplace on the feed streaming across the wall.

That same feed is streaming on Escat's desk. He leaves it running when Raj knocks on his doorframe; when he looks up, his gaze goes first to the satchel Ruby's clutching as though to reassure himself it's still there. Then his attention goes back to the feeds. His body language isn't defensive or wary — he's afraid, but not of them.

It's time to change that.

Raj drops his friendly smile and stalks across the office to Escat's desk, swiping the hologram feed away and spreading his hands in its place. He leans in, forcing Escat to meet his gaze. The director flinches back in his chair and looks to Ruby for help, but her timid inventor's guise has melted away, her shoulders straightening as she pierces Escat with a look of disapproval.

"Director Escat," Raj says, his tone sharp. "I think it's

time we had a frank conversation about what's been going on on this ship."

"What the hell do you think you're doing?" Escat sputters. "I'm calling my security team right now."

"Your security team knows we're here," Raj says. "But we didn't tell them why — out of courtesy to you. If you want to announce you're getting a visit from Federation contraband task force agents, be our guest."

Escat's mouth snaps shut and he straightens in his seat. "No one told me you were coming."

"That's the point, love," Ruby says from her post in the doorway. "You've gotten the heads-up on official visits in the past, have you. But you've been hiding some important details from us, so this time the agency thought we'd have an unannounced poke around."

Guilt flashes over Escat's face; Ruby's guess was a good one.

"You still have friends at the agency." Raj softens his stance, giving Escat more space. A glimmer of hope appears in the other man's eyes, along with a sinking feeling in Raj's stomach. He might have written off Escat's earlier behavior as political sociopathy, but this isn't the body language of a man who ordered Raj and his crew to be killed. They've miscalculated. And Raj has no choice but to continue his ruse and find out everything he can. "Which is why you don't need to be worried — as long as you tell us *everything*."

"That's right," Ruby says. "We would have taken you down already if we thought you *wanted* to work with the Maribi Cartel. We know how they can get their hooks in people."

Now the relief on Escat's face is clear as day — though he doesn't seem quite like a drowning man plucked from the water. More like a man who's just dodged a bullet he knows he deserved. If Raj was betting, he'd put money on the theory that Escat's working relationship with the cartel wasn't forced — at least not at first. If Escat took bribes or agreed to look the other way in exchange for a cut of the cartel's merchandise, it would have meant a small fortune. Of course, the balance of power wouldn't have stayed in Escat's court indefinitely. What had been a windfall at first must now seem like a straitjacket.

And this bastard's greed has put the thousands of people on this ship in danger.

Raj keeps the scorn off his face. Barely.

"Our main concern is getting the cartel off this ship," Raj says. "Start from the beginning. Your friends at the agency can help you if they know exactly what's going on, but if you lie, there won't be anything we can do."

Escat takes a deep breath. "They showed up about six months ago. Threatening people, running drugs — I threatened to call for reinforcements, but their man came to me and said he'd installed a new piece of code in the handshake protocol."

"Malcolm Saint," Raj confirms; Escat nods.

"He said it would let him kill anyone he wanted, and he'd do it if I told anyone he was here." Escat turns to Ruby, face falling with disappointment. "I suppose this means your namidium-finding tech isn't actually real?"

A chill runs down Raj's spine. *Malcolm Saint installed the code in the handshake protocol.*

"Saints in hell," Ruby breathes; Raj leans forward once more, ignoring Escat's comment about the namidium-finding tech.

"Tell us about the handshake code."

CHAPTER 23
JAY

"WHAT'S YOUR PLAN WITH ESCAT?" JAY ASKS MALCOLM; KEEP him talking, he thinks. "I imagine your bosses back at Maribi Station would like to have a few words."

Malcolm inclines his head in confirmation of Jay's guess. "You've probably heard all sorts of nasty things about the Maribi Cartel."

"Rumors get around." Jay shrugs. "I haven't had the pleasure of forming an opinion of my own."

"Rumors especially get around the Pearls," Malcolm says. "They love to hate on the cartels, but who else is going to maintain the infrastructure out here? Oxygen, water, food — if the Federation had its way they'd let us all die."

"I think their resources are limited," Jay says carefully; it's the wrong thing. Snorts of laughter come from Malcolm's crew. The woman with the prosthetic eye gives him a sneer of disgust.

"I've been to Artemis City," Malcolm says. "I've seen the excess. You can't tell me they don't have enough resources."

"Fair." Jay holds his hands up to concede the point. The

kid's not wrong, but it doesn't make whatever he's got in mind right. "What's your plan with Escat?"

"You were right," Malcolm says. "Boss wants to have a word with him, so we're going to take him back to the station. That going to be a problem for you and yours?"

"Not as I see it." And especially not if Escat's the one who tried to kill them. No. The *problem* is this game isn't only between Malcolm and Escat. Given the amount of fire-power Jay saw leave this services hub, Malcolm and his crew are planning to stir up more trouble than a simple kidnapping.

"Glad to hear it," Malcolm says. "Because it'd be awfully hypocritical of you to say otherwise. You and your captain may play at war heroes, but I know the truth."

"Rumors get around about the CLA, too." Jay gives Malcolm a tight smile; he's not interested in rehashing who committed which atrocities with a kid who runs drugs for a living. "And winners write the history books."

"I'm not talking about the CLA, I'm talking about Nico Garnet." Malice glitters in Malcolm's hazel eyes. "I've heard rumors about him, too."

Jay keeps his expression neutral. "Garnet?"

"You stood out when we met," Malcolm says. "Your accent, of course, but it wasn't just that you're a long way from home. I did some searching and found out that ship used to belong to Nico Garnet."

"Used to, sure. Doesn't anymore, though." And he, Ruby, and Gracie did an awful lot of work to keep that from being apparent to the casual observer. Malcolm or his people might have recognized Jay or Lasadi from a past Garnet job, but there's no way they should recognize the *Nanshe*.

"You didn't delete the core logs," Malcolm says with a cold smile, and Jay's stomach drops.

The work they did would have kept the *Nanshe*'s identity a secret from visual identification, and from the handshake code. Of course they hadn't deleted the history at the core of the *Nanshe*'s system — because you'd only find it if you had top-level access to that data.

And to the core overrides.

This means one thing, and Malcolm wants him to know exactly what it is.

"You're the one who hacked our system."

"I didn't realize you worked for the Garnets until after I sent the order to override your safety protocols. Escat was looking for a way out, and I was trying to keep him in line."

"Ah. Makes it all good, then." Jay's tone is mild, but anger simmers not far from the surface; the toughs surrounding him shift warily, but Malcolm doesn't seem bothered.

"History gone and dusted now, though." Malcolm's smile is knife sharp. "Now it's profitable for us to work together. But if profit isn't motivating, remember the lives of your crew are in my hands. I frankly don't care why you help me, I only know you will. Come."

Malcolm turns to leave, and by the half-dozen weapons that lift around him, Jay doesn't have much of a choice but to follow. The woman with the prosthetics grabs his arm; he shakes her off with an angry curse. He may not be free to go, but he's damn well not going to be carried.

They head back towards the marketplace, passing through empty corridors and services hubs. The dark energy coursing through the ship has gone before them; anyone who doesn't have a strong reason to be out in public has found a place to shelter. Rather than joining whatever fray the Maribi Cartel is stirring up in the marketplace, though, Malcolm stops at a door between two shower facilities in the Module E services hub where he and Jay first met. The table where they'd played those hands of mystix is abandoned, the stasis field sizzling as it glitches.

The door Malcolm has stopped in front of is marked Staff Only. Jay had noticed it earlier, but assumed it was some sort of utilities closet. Instead, when Malcolm swipes his credentials, the door opens to reveal a maintenance shaft stretching out about ten meters. An access airlock is built into one side, and the far end is capped by a door like the one Malcolm just opened.

Jay struggles to remember the hologram of the *Slingshot* they'd studied before they docked, wishing he had Alex's photographic memory to help him out. If he recalls correctly, each passenger and docking module is self-sufficient so they can be swapped out for repairs and be maneuvered individually if needed. Which meant each module has . . .

"That's the control unit," Jay says.

Malcolm winks at Jay and floats into the shaft, followed by one of the burly brothers. The other gestures for Jay to follow, then takes up the rear. The two women and the man with the snake tattoo on his throat take up defensive positions in the services hub itself.

Malcolm's credentials get them into the control unit as easily as they got them into the shaft, and Jay takes a lungful of stale, dusty air. Been a while since someone came out here, he'd guess. Even longer than it's been since someone cleaned the rehydrator in the communal kitchen. He spins slowly to take it all in.

The control unit is about as big as the *Nanshe*'s galley. It's depressingly utilitarian, every surface spray-coated with an anticorrosive, antibacterial rubber in the same greenish-gray hue, sickly orange emergency lights casting harsh shadows, but there's nothing special about the layout. Jay's worked on municipal contractor tech, back on Corusca with his father. He's worked on the Teguçan military tech the CLA used to fight the Alliance. He's worked on the *Nanshe*; Mapalad's an Artemisian company. The labels and positions of the controls all may be a little differ-ent, but the general principle is the same — and this *Sling-shot* control unit is no different.

Malcolm turns to Jay, an arm's length away. The unit's meant for a small crew, but the two burly brothers and their weapons soak up the space and make it feel claustrophobic. "You know how to make one of these work?"

"This is a Bast-Lev unit, right? Bixian manufacturer, they specialize in long-haulers."

Malcolm and his crew exchange a glance that says they don't have a clue. Jay continues on.

"BLs aren't designed for flashy flying, they're meant to be run by anyone. Good guidance AI, automated anti-asteroid defenses, foolproof autopilot, instruction manual with lots of pictures. The operator is basically here to keep the systems running." Jay shrugs. "In other words, anyone can fly it once it's turned on."

"And how do we get it turned on?"

"That's the easy part. It's a subordinate unit, designed to come online as soon as it realizes it's been cut off from the rest of the ship. Decoupling it will be the challenge." Jay takes a deep breath. "You're not just after Escat, you're here to steal the ship."

Malcolm smiles. "Not all of it."

"Federation probably won't care you only hijacked part of the *Slingshot*."

"We've got an insurance plan."

"Escat? And then what, Malcolm? You're going to leave a bunch of your fellow Belters drifting in space without their ships? You know people in the marketplace will be stranded — most of them have ships docked in this section. You were talking a big game about doing this for the greater good. The greater good of everyone in the Belt? Or the greater good of the Maribi Cartel?"

Malcolm's nostrils flare. "I wouldn't worry about who I

work for," he says. "I would worry more about yourself. Unless you'd prefer to be stranded here with everyone else."

"You're saying that if I help you, my crew and I can take our ship and go."

"I have no need of your ship. And I'd rather have allies who want to keep the Alliance out of the black. I assumed if you had the moral flexibility to work with Nico Garnet, you wouldn't have such a problem working with me."

Jay takes a sharp breath. "Again, I can't make this call alone."

"Then talk to your captain." When Jay hesitates, Malcolm smiles. "Or are you afraid of what her orders might be?"

Jay won't admit it to this asshole, but that's exactly what's causing him to hesitate. He knows what *he* would do: he would fight like hell to make sure Malcolm doesn't get away with his plan. But Las? She'll probably see the stolen ships as material loss, not worth risking any of their lives over — but for too many of the *Slingshot*'s passengers, losing their ship means losing their livelihood. They're all living so close to the brink, it's as good as a death sentence.

But this isn't just Jay's decision. He pulls out his comm.

"Las, hey. We've got another problem."

"You're still with Saint?"

"Yeah. Right next to him."

"Are you hurt?"

"No. Las — "

"It's the bastard's lucky day, then. Put me on broadcast."

There's so much he'd say if Malcolm wasn't standing right here, but any errant word now will give the other man more fodder. *Dammit, Las, don't let me down.* Jay takes a deep breath, hits Broadcast. "You're good."

"Saint." The word cuts through the stuffy interior of the control unit like a blade. Lasadi might not sound angry to most people, but Jay knows the amount of cold fury hidden beneath the surface when she takes that tone. "I don't take kindly to people who try to kill my crew and threaten my friends. We know about the handshake code."

"Trying to kill you was an error," Malcolm says. "And I apologize. I didn't realize you were affiliated with the Garnets."

"Tora Garnet generally doesn't accept 'I killed your people by accident' to be an apology. But she's not here right now."

"She's not." And by Malcolm's expression, he doesn't much care what Tora Garnet does and does not accept. Tora's name might carry enough weight to make Jay and the others useful right now — it won't keep them safe for long.

"We've made contact with Escat," Lasadi says, and Jay's heart sinks. "What do you need next?"

"There's a shuttle docked in his unit. Bring him there, my people will meet you."

"Done."

"Las." Jay ignores Malcolm's arched eyebrow. "We can't just hand Escat over."

"Number one priority is keeping you safe and getting back to our ship."

Frustration flares through him. "And the people on the *Slingshot*?"

"Aren't our problem."

"You can't be fucking serious."

"That's an order, Kamiya." Lasadi's tone is cold, dispassionate. "Do what Saint says, and trust me."

She cuts the connection, and the sudden stuffy silence in the control unit closes back around him. Jay's an arm's length from Malcolm. He could grab that plasma pistol from Malcolm's hip, maybe even disable him before one of the bruiser brothers got a shot off. But that's where the fight would end — he can't take the two brothers at once, and even if he could, three of Malcolm's crew are waiting outside.

Malcolm's watching him, amusement in his eyes.

Trust me, Lasadi said.

It's not like Jay has a choice.

"Sounds like you have your orders, my friend," Malcolm says. "Let's get this module decoupled."

CHAPTER 24
RAJ

THE WAY ESCAT'S BEEN TELLING IT TO RAJ AND RUBY, HE'S just another innocent bystander taken in by the ruthless Maribi Cartel. His sob story is this: They installed a flea in the handshake code without Escat's knowledge, which gave them deadly control over every ship docked on the *Slingshot*, which effectively tied Escat's hands. This let the cartel use the *Slingshot* as their own personal recruiting grounds and trafficking highway, and Escat couldn't do a thing about it without risking the lives of his passengers.

Which, Escat wants them to know, was his highest priority.

Raj has been half listening as Escat spills his story, mostly because he doesn't entirely believe the director when he claims his hands are completely clean. Escat's been living comfortably for a while, and not on his mining operations and government salary. The Maribi Cartel would have approached Escat with a pair of golden handcuffs that probably didn't look so deadly at the beginning. And Escat seems like the sort of man who would have put them on willingly.

Even if Raj's hunch is true, though, he's not here to assign blame. He's here to save lives.

"What else does Saint have access to?" Raj asks, cutting Escat's excuses off.

Escat swallows. "Um . . ." He either doesn't know or he's preparing to lie, and either way they're running out of time. Raj motions Ruby forward.

"Up you go," she says, crossing to Escat's desk and shooing him from his seat with a little wave. "Let us have a look."

"You can't," Escat sputters. "This is high-clearance information."

"And what level of security clearance do you think we have at the agency?" Ruby holds Escat's gaze with an arched eyebrow until he finally stands, then settles into his chair while he hovers awkwardly beside her. Red-lacquered fingernails clatter against the desk; Ruby swipes open Escat's deleted messages folder, pulls up the one Escat supposedly sent to his head of security right before the attack on the *Nanshe*. "You sent this, love, did you."

Escat frowns, reading over her shoulder. "'Please pacify Berth 32,'" he reads aloud. "I have no idea what this means."

Raj believes him this time. "It's the message that was sent right before someone hacked our ship's overrides and tried to poison us all."

The color washes from Escat's face. "I didn't know," he says. "You have to believe me."

"Then how did Saint fake your login and biosign?" Raj asks.

"He made me give him access."

"And you did, because he was holding the rest of the passengers hostage."

"That's what he told me," Escat says, voice hoarse. "He

said he could kill anyone he wanted and make it look like an accident. I didn't think it was true at first, but then . . ."

"Then he killed Karl Gatmaitan," Raj guesses. Escat nods, lips pressed into a thin line. "He made it look like there was a problem with his ship, and you marked it as a heart attack so nobody would look into it further."

"How do you know about Karl?"

"We found your correspondence," Raj says. Ruby's still frowning at the desk, having swiped away Escat's messages and dug deeper into the system hunting gods know what — Raj can't make sense of the rapid flash of data, file structures, and schematics. "You were talking about going into business together."

"I thought if I got some extra money I could buy Saint out, get him off the ship for good," Escat says. "But then Saint found out — I'll admit, I wasn't taking him seriously until then."

"He's definitely to be taken seriously." Ruby sits back suddenly, expression grim. "Because he's about to do something incredibly stupid. He's in the control unit in Module E. He's going to try to uncouple the *Slingshot* at the marketplace."

Escat shakes his head. "He can't do that."

"I think he can, love. If you gave Saint the ability to fake your login and biosign, he can do anything he wants."

"No," Escat says. "I mean, the modules can't be safely decoupled without going through the proper procedure from both sides of the unit. If he forces the action from Module E, it could cause a chain reaction that destroys the entire marketplace module."

"Either Saint doesn't know or he doesn't care," Ruby says. "Because that's exactly what he's about to do."

Raj's earpiece crackles to life with Lasadi's voice. "Raj, Ruby, come in."

Raj and Ruby exchange a look; he points to the desk.

"Figure out how to stop him, and start evacuating everyone into the first-class section. I'll be right back." He steps outside the office to take Lasadi's call. Escat's aide is still sitting near the door, glued to the feeds from the marketplace; he flicks Raj a worried look, then turns back to stare at the chaos streaming across his desk. "We've got some bad news," Raj says.

"Me, too. You go first."

"Saint is trying to decouple the *Slingshot* at the marketplace, and Escat tells us that could cause a chain reaction that could destroy the marketplace module."

"We need to evacuate, then."

"We're on it."

"And figure out how to keep Saint from initiating the decoupling process — I've got an idea of how to get to him if you can do that." She takes a deep breath. "My turn for bad news — we're out of time. Saint is ready for Escat, he said take him to the shuttle in the director's unit. He has some people waiting there."

Raj glances back inside the office. Ruby is typing furiously, Escat is offering guidance over her shoulder. The director looks ill with worry. "Are we really giving this guy to Saint?"

"Do you see a way around it?"

Raj closes his eyes, trying to think. When he opens them again, Escat's aide is still watching the feeds, worrying a pen in his fingers. The man fumbles it when he catches Raj's eye, and it goes clattering across the desktop and onto the floor. "I might have an idea. Las, we'll worry about evacuating the marketplace. Get yourself out of there."

"I have something to do first," she says, and a fist clenches around his heart. "I'll make it fast."

CHAPTER 25
LASADI

"You've got a lot of experience with apologies, right?" Lasadi asks Alex. She edges between two halves of a bickering couple to grasp the lip of one of the marketplace's platforms and pull herself farther into the crowd. The swarm of bodies has gotten thicker in the past ten minutes, and meaner.

Alex pulls himself after her, agile as a cat. "I'm a pro."

"How do I explain to Fiona we are not the bad guys without telling her what's going on?"

"Ooh, tough one." Alex pivots past an old man, tapping his fingers on his lips in thought. "Basically, quote, 'I have a perfectly good explanation for all this, but I can't tell you so you'll have to trust me.' That's a master's-level non-apology, though. It requires a lot of nuance — and time."

"Any ideas for something simpler?" Lasadi elbows past a large man in a tattered jumpsuit, who yells a curse after her. She ignores him.

"Hmm. I don't personally have a lot of experience with *this* genre of apology, but you might try the truth? Like, you screwed up and don't really have an excuse, but that doesn't matter because the bigger point is a bunch of people are about to die?" Alex shrugs. "It's direct and gets to the point."

"The truth is good." Lasadi kicks off a table, aiming for a gap in the crowd; she can spot Fiona hanging back from the chaos, guarding her stall. The other woman hasn't spotted her yet. "But is it believable?"

"Third option: You blame it all on me. That costs you, though."

Lasadi lifts an eyebrow at Alex. "It costs me?"

"I have reasonable rates and good references. I've taken the fall for classmates tons of times — the ayas always assumed anything bad happening at the convent was my fault anyways, so eventually I started making money off it."

"Very entrepreneurial."

"Thanks."

"But I think I'll go for option two."

"Probably a good call."

Lasadi pushes her way past the last dregs of protesters to Fiona's stall. Fiona's eyes narrow when she approaches.

"I thought I said I never wanted to see you again." Fiona sets her jaw. "I've got enough problems."

"I can explain, but we don't have much time." Lasadi waves a hand at the gathering crowd around them. "All this? The cartel is planning on hijacking part of the *Slingshot*, and they set this protest up as a distraction. They're going to decouple the marketplace unit unless we stop them — which will cause a chain reaction and blow up everything in here. Including us."

"I don't know what you're selling now, but you can go find another patsy."

"I'm not selling anything."

"Then who the hell are you?"

Olds, but what's the fastest way through this conversation? A dozen lies flash through Lasadi's mind, but only one thing has a chance of convincing Fiona. The truth.

"Do the names Vash and Gracie mean anything to you?"

Fiona straightens; that's a yes.

"They're friends. They asked us to come investigate Karl's death, but we didn't know who to trust."

"Then what was all that business with the namidium?"

"A way to get the director's attention. You're right, it was bullshit of us to get people's hopes up. But we never intended to scam anyone but him."

Fiona gnaws on the inside of her cheek, clearly wavering between wanting to believe Lasadi and wanting to tell her to get the hell out of her sight.

"I'm sorry," Lasadi says quietly.

Fiona takes a deep breath. "Karl used to talk about Vash and Gracie all the time," she says after a moment. "If you'd been honest with me from the beginning, I would've told you anything you wanted to know."

"I can see that now." Lasadi holds Fiona's gaze. "Look, I can't make up for the fact that we lied to you, but know we've always been on your side. And people are going to die if we don't act fast."

"And why should I believe you now?"

"You just have to believe yourself," Lasadi says. "Do you think the cartel is capable of this or not?"

Fiona nods slowly. "I heard some of them talking the other day. I thought it was a couple of kids bullshitting, only, talking about stealing the *Slingshot*. It can't be possible."

"It's not only possible, it's about to happen."

There's been a textural shift in the background noise of the crowd, a new voice booming through the chatter, someone screaming back responses. Lasadi can't make out the words, can't see who's causing the new ruckus. Is it Escat's security team trying to begin an evacuation? The cartel members stirring up even more trouble?

She turns back to Fiona, urgent. "I'm sorry I can't explain more, but we don't have time. Will you help me?"

Fiona's teeth catch her bottom lip one last time as she scans the crowd with worry, then she breathes deep and squares her shoulders, turning her attention to Lasadi. "What can I do to help?"

"People here trust you. Will they follow your directions?"

"I still see a few people here I can talk sense into. They can help me with the others."

"Good. If you can handle things in here, Alex and I will take care of the rest." She glances over her shoulder at him. "Do you have everything we need?"

"Almost," Alex says. He smiles brightly at Fiona. "You sell mining supplies, right?"

"Yes?"

"Perfect."

Lasadi pulls out her comm, swiping credits over to Fiona. The other woman's eyes widen at the amount. "Alex might need to do a little shopping first," Lasadi says. "Let me tell you the plan."

CHAPTER 26
JAY

"I THOUGHT YOU SAID YOU WERE FAMILIAR WITH THESE UNITS." Malcolm's words are followed by the sharp rap of his thumb against the control panel. He doesn't seem to have noticed his own gesture, but it's not the first time he's done it.

His perfectly cool facade has held up this long, but now his tells are starting to show. The unconscious rap of the thumb, the twitch in the cheek, the flared nostrils — Malcolm's getting anxious as the minutes stretch on. He's issued the order for Lasadi to bring Escat to the shuttle, but he hasn't gotten confirmation that the director is there yet, and Jay is taking longer than he'd like to feel his way through the decoupling protocol. Not all evil plans can go off perfectly without a hitch, Jay supposes.

"I'm familiar with how the control unit operates mechanically." Jay waves a hand at the panel in front of him; he's pulled up the densely worded documentation manual and is trying to decipher it. "It's the software interface that's moxed. But I think I can't force the decoupling process from one side without an override from the director himself. So we'll have to wait for him."

"Why didn't you say so?" Malcolm snaps. He leans over and enters a code, then presses his palm to the screen. It blinks green

CREDENTIALS ACCEPTED: DANIEL ESCAT

"There. Keep working."

"Fancy." Jay frowns at the new options unlocked by Malcolm's false credentials. Something doesn't feel right, but the user interface is counterintuitive and he's having trouble grasping it. Old ones, but he's not a hacker, why does he have to keep telling people this? "Just tell me what does *what*," he mutters under his breath as he opens up a menu labeled Maintenance. A warning pops onto the screen.

MANUAL OVERRIDE DETECTED FOR MAINTENANCE OPTIONS. ABORT OR CONTINUE Y/N? CAUTION ADVISED.

Is he being advised against continuing with the manual override? Or against aborting it? And which option — abort or continue — does hitting Yes choose?

"Who designed this fucking thing?" he asks, scanning through the documentation manual with his finger hovering between Yes and No.

"I believe we want Yes," Malcolm says, but he doesn't sound any more certain than Jay. "Hold on, though. I need confirmation your friends have delivered Escat before we initiate the decoupling." Malcolm leans back in his chair, studying Jay. "You don't seem too happy about that."

"Can't say I like kidnapping."

"I wouldn't be concerned with what happens to a man like Director Escat. Whatever he tells you, he built his bed with the Maribi Cartel years ago, and his debt has come due. I'm sure you've collected your share of debts for Nico Garnet."

"We owed him a debt of our own."

"Your captain doesn't seem to care about Escat."

"She and I don't always see eye to eye."

"And yet you follow her."

Jay shrugs. "Never met anyone I see eye to eye with one hundred percent of the time. Have you?"

"I suppose not." Malcolm flicks his thumb unconsciously against the desk once more, that muscle jumping in his cheek again. "Get me the feed from the marketplace."

"Sure thing." Jay knows this one, at least — the camera feeds are clearly labeled, unlike the rest of the nonsense on the control panel. He hits the one marked Marketplace and throws it up on the wall behind the desk.

It takes Jay a moment to understand what's happening.

The view it gives them is from the top of the marketplace, he thinks, the camera pointing down to give a wide-angle look at the chaos below. Normally, that would make it easy to see nearly everything happening in the module, but now the screen is filled with people. The marketplace is packed, and starting to get violent. As Jay watches, two people charge a security guard and try to wrestle away the guard's weapon. The other security guards are ready for them, though. One of the attackers gets slammed in the face with the butt of a stun carbine, the other arches back as an electric barb hooks into his thigh. Their bodies drift in the neutral zone between the protesters and the pack of security guards and — for the moment, at least — no one else attempts an attack.

Malcolm slams his palm on the desk. "What is taking so long," he growls.

Either Escat is giving Lasadi trouble, or she's stalling, Jay realizes. And if it's the latter, it's only a matter of time before Malcolm begins to get suspicious of her.

"You asked earlier why I was so bothered by my captain working with you, if we'd worked with Nico Garnet," Jay says. It's not exactly what Malcolm had asked, but the question seems to intrigue him; his hand stills on the desktop. "I think it's exactly because of Garnet. It started out as a debt, but the woman I used to follow into battle never would have kept working for the Garnets for so long past when her debt was paid. And now?" Jay shrugs. "I thought she was still recovering from the war, you know? I thought she just needed time, and she'd come back to being the person I once respected. But this is proving me wrong."

"Most people would be happy knowing their friends would do anything to get them back."

"My old captain would have done what's right, not sacrificed Escat and used me like a pawn." Jay doesn't bother to keep the bitterness out of his tone; it's not a stretch of the imagination to pretend these words are real.

Malcolm's watching him, curious. "What keeps you with her?"

"Never quite found the right reason to leave, I guess."

Before Malcolm can answer, his comm chimes. He glances at the screen, then his shoulders relax. "She delivered Escat," he says. Jay takes a sharp, involuntary breath; Malcolm laughs. "Found your reason to leave, I think."

"Maybe I have," Jay says, but his mind is no longer on distracting Malcolm to give Lasadi time for whatever it is she's planning. His unconscious has been puzzling over the user interface and the poorly written documentation manual glowing beside the blinking warning light on the desk. It's finally dawned on him what the clunky user interface is trying to explain.

"Malcolm." Jay grabs the other man's arm, ignoring the bristling weapons of the bruiser brothers behind them. "Listen to me."

"What is it?"

"This isn't going to work. You need to initiate the decoupling sequence from both modules, not just this one."

"We can manually override that safeguard. I have the director's credentials."

"Not without risking failure in the other module. I can

take care of it, easy, but I have to be in the other module. Send me with your guys if you want, but if you don't go through the proper process you could kill a bunch of people."

He expects surprise or worry — even disbelief. But Malcolm Saint gives him a chilling smile.

"You can't do this," Jay says desperately. "You wanted help, and I can help you. But there's a thousand people on board this ship. Hundreds in that marketplace module. You keep talking about how this is the heart of the Belt — do you really not give a shit what happens to them?"

"They've all had a chance to choose whether to side with the Belt or with the Pearls. I offered them protection. I can't save anyone who doesn't want to be saved."

"You can start by not killing them."

Malcolm lifts his comm, opening up a channel; by the corresponding chime from the comms of the two bruiser brothers, Jay guesses it's an open call to everyone on his crew.

"Brace yourselves," Malcolm says. "It's time."

One of the brothers grabs Jay from behind as he tries to lunge, muscle-clad arms pinning him to the chair. Malcolm leans forward to key in the override code once more.

MANUAL OVERRIDE ACCEPTED. INITIATE DECOUPLE?

Malcolm hits Yes; the desk glows red with warning.

"What have you done?" Jay asks, but Malcolm doesn't answer.

The control unit shudders around them with a lurch that throws the bruisers back and knocks Malcolm from his chair. Jay clutches the edge of the control panel to keep from flying across the unit, but he can't see any way to cancel the disaster Malcolm has initiated.

And even if he could, it's too late.

The marketplace feed above the desk shows pure panic, bodies shoving against each other and into the camera itself as the feed shakes violently. Someone goes flying towards the screen and bounces off, ricocheting back into the crowd with their limbs limp.

The data streaming across the control panel is absolutely horrifying. The decoupling was a success, but as Jay had predicted, it caused a chain reaction that sparked an explosion at the entryway to the marketplace — and that is only the beginning. Jay watches in horror as the decoupled part of the *Slingshot* begins to return frantic failure notices. Emergency systems light up, reporting that the marketplace module will be sealed off even as the module's life support systems begin to shut down. Even as fire begins to spread.

There's nothing Jay can do but watch helplessly as smoke pours into the screen, then sparks; the control unit shudders around Jay with the force of another, bigger explosion.

The feed from the marketplace goes black.

CHAPTER 27
JAY

Jay grabs on to the arms of the chair to keep from being thrown loose, hooks his foot into the security bar jutting from the floor, and uses it to lever himself back into the seat. His hands hover over the controls, numb. Behind him, the two bruiser brothers are regaining their footing. Malcolm floats nearby, having been shaken from his own seat by the second blast. Jay ignores them all.

Lasadi. He has to get through to Lasadi.

Jay fumbles for his comm, fingers stabbing for the connection, but it keeps bouncing back. Nonemergency communications have been shut down, Jay tells himself. The shattered system isn't letting signals through, but Lasadi and the others *must* be headed back to the *Nanshe*. They'll have gotten there by now, and they're waiting for him.

He can't let any other explanation for the silence enter his mind.

The control panel blinks with a distress signal from the other half of the *Slingshot*; Jay reaches to play it, but Malcolm cuts it off after the first few automated words echo through the control unit. His expression is eerily calm.

"There are other ships in the area to help them," he says. "It's time for us to make our exit."

Jay shakes his head; there's no other ship remotely big enough to help the *Slingshot* — assuming anyone in the other half survived the blast. "I need to know if my crew is still alive."

"They are if they were smart," Malcolm says. "They had plenty of warning. But if they were trying to be heroes, I can't make any promises."

Let them have been smart, not heroes.

The thought shoots rebellious through Jay's mind, and despite all the arguments he's had with Lasadi, despite all the mostly truths he told Malcolm a moment ago, now he's desperately hoping she decided not to stick her neck out and endanger her crew. Please, let her have selfishly delivered Escat to the cartel and gotten her ass back on the *Nanshe*.

"I need to hear from them," Jay says. He slips his feet from under the security bar, shifts subtly in his seat. "You don't need me to fly this thing — I already told you it more or less takes care of itself. But it's going to take you some time to figure it out, and if we want to escape the debris field from the explosion, we need to act fast."

Malcolm arches an eyebrow at him. "What happened to giving a shit about saving the people on this ship?"

"I need to know what happened to my crew," Jay says. "That's all I give a shit about right now."

Malcolm turns to issue an order to one of the brothers, and Jay doesn't know — or care — whether he's about to tell the bruiser to make contact with Lasadi or to shoot Jay and take over flying the control unit. The important thing is that Malcolm has turned his back.

Jay launches himself from the chair, boots kicking off the dashboard to slam his shoulder into Malcolm. The kid's magboots weren't locked to the floor, so the momentum sends them both crashing into the nearest brother.

Jay wrenches himself around in midair, one arm around Malcolm's neck, pulling the other man's body in front of his to block a direct attack from the brothers. He grabs for Malcolm's plasma pistol from its holster while Malcolm struggles in his grasp.

Before Jay can draw the weapon, though, Malcolm's foot finds contact with something sturdy and he kicks, sending them both spinning into the wall above the desk. The plasma pistol goes flying, ricocheting off the ceiling before Jay loses sight of it.

Jay absorbs the impact with his shoulder and rolls, but Malcolm's taken advantage of the momentum to pull free. He locks his magboots on the wall and yanks Jay's arm with all his might; Jay crashes past him, elbows up to protect his head as his back smashes a monitor into a shower of sparks.

His only hope is to keep moving.

He rolls out of the way as one of the brothers fires at him, a blast of heat searing the wall beside the monitor where Jay's head had just been.

"Don't shoot!" Malcolm yells. "We'll be fucking dead in the black."

Jay takes advantage of the moment's distraction to wrench a canister of fire suppressant from the wall and brace himself, throwing it at the closest bruiser brother. The man grunts in pain when it glances off his shoulder; his brother ducks as the canister ricochets towards his head.

Jay launches himself at the ceiling before Malcolm can grab for him, catching hold of a strap and using it to spin a kick that catches the first brother in the jaw. The bruiser's head snaps up, blood droplets trickling from his mouth, eyes rolling back in his head. He begins to drift.

No time to celebrate — the second brother's hands close

around Jay's leg like a vise as Jay tries to twist away. The brother locks his magboots to the floor and powers down into a squat, tearing Jay from his grip on the ceiling strap and sending him crashing into the chair in front of the control panel.

Jay shakes stars out of his eyes as the brother grabs him from behind, then shoves off the chair to crack the back of his head into the place where the brother's nose should be. He's rewarded by a yowl of pain, but the arms around his chest stay bands of iron, and the magboots locking them both in place make him a sitting target when Malcolm decks him across the face.

Pain explodes through Jay's left cheek.

Malcolm's second blow catches Jay dead in the stomach. Jay gasps for breath; when he blinks his vision clear, his lashes are sticky with blood.

"Your friends are dead." Malcolm catches Jay with another hook to the gut; Jay doubles over, tastes blood. "And so are you."

"Fuck you."

Malcolm's face contorts with anger and he rears back for a bigger punch — Jay shoves back against the brother and kicks up with all his strength, catching Malcolm in the chest with his boots and using that as a launch point to continue his momentum. The movement wrenches him free from the brother's grip, somersaulting him backwards.

Jay's ribs are screaming and he can't control his rotation as much as he'd like, so he hits the ceiling back first, unable to do more than drift, all his momentum absorbed by the crash landing. He wipes the back of one hand across his eye; it comes away slick with blood, but that's not the most important thing at the moment.

The important thing is that the fingers of his other hand have closed around the grip of Malcolm's errant plasma pistol.

Jay braces himself and twists to find Malcolm, squeezing the trigger without caring anymore what important part of the ship he might hit. But someone grabs his foot and the shot goes wild, searing across the control panel in a shower of sparks that obscure Malcolm. Malcolm lunges for the door.

Wherever he's going, Jay has to stop him. He tries to kick away from the brother's grip on his ankle, but pain sears up his back. He turns back to find the other brother grinning at him, blood on his teeth.

"Where do you think you're going?"

The brother raises his stun baton again.

Jay fires.

CHAPTER 28
LASADI

"You know Jay trained me to shoot a pistol." Alex says. He holds up the electric barb Lasadi gave him with a skeptical look. "I mean, if you want some real backup in there."

The light in the airlock blinks green and Lasadi unseals her helmet; it folds back into her collar. "I believe you, but I also promised your sister you're not here to fight."

The blast charges Alex detonated on the outside of the control unit seem to have done their work, and Ruby's been sending fake emergency signals to complete the ruse. Fiona's charade with her friends on the marketplace video feeds should be the icing on the cake to convince Saint that his plan worked.

Lasadi glances at Alex. "Stay behind me and let me take care of things."

"What Ruby doesn't know won't hurt her."

"You do know I can hear you," Ruby says through the comms. "And the captain is absolutely right. Stay behind her and stay safe. Airlock's good to go when you are. Remember, you'll have the advantage on Saint's people, but not for long."

"Love you too, sis." Alex shoots Lasadi a grin, but it's

thin, papering over nerves. Of course, it would be troubling if Alex *didn't* seem nervous. The first time Lasadi went into combat, it had been behind the controls of a ship rather than charging out of an airlock with a weapon in her hand — but the gravitas of the situation had still made her shaky. Fortunately, Jay had been there at her back. Whether he'd sensed her nerves or just needed to get his own fears out in the open, he'd been the first one to speak.

"Please tell me I'm not the only one who's scared as hell," he'd said, and relief had flooded through Lasadi.

"Definitely not."

Jay had started laughing from his seat behind her, and something about his laugh had drained the rest of her fear. "Thank the old ones," he'd said. "I wasn't going to be able to handle it if you were really as superhumanly cool as you looked."

They'd come back from that mission together — and so many others after it. And they'll come back from this one, too. If the Alliance couldn't take Jay away from her, there's no way some two-bit cartel hoodlum is going to.

"Stay sharp," Lasadi tells Alex. "You've got this." Alex returns her solemn nod, and Lasadi hits the button to open the airlock door.

They've entered the access shaft between the services hub and the control unit in Module E. The airlock is closer to the services hub, and that door is wide open, which means Lasadi will need to take out the members of Saint's crew waiting there before she can get to Jay in the control unit.

There are three of them inside the door: a woman with a wicked-looking eye implant, a man with a snake tattooed around his throat, and a small woman with a long blond braid that whips around her shoulders when she spins to see Lasadi.

Lasadi fires on her while she's still going for her

weapon, hitting her square in the chest with a blast from her stun carbine. The blond woman flies back with a yelp, arms flung wide and magboots fried by the pulse. Lasadi's second shot hits the tattooed man in the shoulder; he grunts in pain, but still manages to swing his weapon her way.

"Stay here!" Lasadi shouts, but Alex is already moving. Lasadi launches herself out of the way of the snake man's blast, aiming for the cover of an overturned table and firing his way as she somersaults.

She'd hoped Alex would stay in the access shaft; instead she lands to find him pirouetting through the air with an acrobat's grace. He's not headed for cover. No. He's flying directly into the line of fire of the woman with the eye implant.

Lasadi watches in horror as the woman pulls the trigger — and as Alex whips impossibly in a new direction in midair, cartwheeling towards the ceiling, where he lands gracefully, slightly above and behind the woman. He locks his magboots and backbends like a reed, firing his electric barb at her neck.

The woman with the implants goes limp.

Lasadi is so shocked she nearly lets herself get hit by the next bolt from Snake Man's gun. She ducks just in time, launching herself from her cover to plow knees-first into his sternum. She wraps her arm around his throat and pivots behind him, slapping a tranquility patch on his neck with her free hand. She growls out a curse as his fingers dig painfully into the meat of her forearm, but keeps her grip until he finally stops struggling.

Lasadi releases him and pushes his body to drift gently across the room, using the opposite momentum to send herself towards the floor. Her magboots click into place.

She looks up to find Alex grinning at her from the ceiling.

"You'll have to teach me that trick," Lasadi says.

"Happy to, Cap."

"Secure these guys," she tells Alex. "I don't want them waking up to come after me."

If he chafes at being told to stay behind once more, she doesn't see it. She's already soaring back through the access shaft towards the control unit.

The door's open now — did they hear the scuffle in the services hub and come to investigate? Lasadi's heart lurches when she hears Jay's scream of agony, then the sharp sizzle of a plasma pistol.

She can't see a thing through the door, it's choked with smoke from an electrical fire, but the fire suppression system is whirring to clear out the air. Lasadi holds her stun carbine in front of her, advancing as the smoke clears.

The first thing she sees is the bodies: A pair of burly men who look like brothers are both floating near the doorway. One looks like he's unconscious, but the other has a smoking hole in his chest. Behind the bodies, a lanky figure whirls with a pistol in his hand.

He drops it to his side when he sees who she is.

"Las," Jay breathes. "You're alive."

"We're all okay." She lowers her stun carbine, but doesn't drop it entirely. There should have been a fourth person in this room. "Where's Malcolm."

"He went out the door you came in."

"I didn't see him. Are you okay?"

He doesn't answer her question; Lasadi suspects he doesn't know yet. Whatever happened to him, he looks like hell. His left eye is swelling and smeared with blood and there's a vicious-looking gash on his bicep, weeping fat crimson beads into the air.

"We need to get you to a doctor."

"We don't have time. We need to stop Malcolm — because if you didn't see him, then he went outside the ship."

"The airlock."

"Exactly."

"Then he'll definitely see he was played."

"What do you mean?"

"The explosion was fake," Lasadi says. "He didn't manage to decouple the ship — we just made it look that way to buy us time to get over here."

Jay's bloodshot eyes meet hers, sparking with hope he doesn't quite seem to believe. "It felt so real."

"That was Alex. He rigged up detonating blasts around the control unit."

"Clever," Jay says. "Where did he get that idea?"

"He said it was inspired by you."

"Seems like I'm being a bad influence on the kid."

"Corrupt him all you want," Lasadi says. "It's working out pretty well for the rest of us."

Jay's smile fades. "I need to get to Malcolm."

"You're in no shape for that."

"Do you know how to repair a decoupling unit?"

"Jay . . ."

She wants to try to stop him, to take care of this herself and send him back to the *Nanshe* so he can get his injuries checked. But she knows he won't go. More than that, she knows he's right. If Saint has gone to decouple the ship from the other side, then she's definitely not going to be able to stop him on her own.

"I'm going with you."

Jay shakes his head. "I need you in the *Nanshe*."

Lasadi takes a sharp breath. "Fine. What's your plan?"

"I have no idea." Jay runs a hand through his shaggy black hair, pushing it out of his eyes. His fingers come away streaked with blood. "Help me into one of those environment suits and let's come up with something together."

CHAPTER 29
JAY

THE ENVIRONMENT SUIT STARTS WITH THE WARNING BELLS AS soon as Jay zips it up. His blood pressure is too high. His stress hormones are spiked. He's bleeding in multiple places, despite Las's quick patch job on the gash on his arm. When it asks him if he wants an emergency stim pack, he hits Yes gratefully; needles pierce his neck, followed by an ebb in the pain.

Ought to keep him going for a little bit longer. Hopefully for as long as he needs to stop Malcolm from *actually* destroying the *Slingshot* and everybody else on it.

He hadn't quite believed Lasadi when she told him they'd faked blowing up the marketplace, not until the airlock opened and he saw it with his own eyes. Instead of a breached unit and a sea of bodies scattering into the black, the marketplace module is intact. The control unit he'd been stuck in with Malcolm is painted with scorch marks from the detonating blasts Alex and Lasadi planted.

Everything is all right — for now. It's up to Jay to make sure it stays that way. He checks the straps of his tool pack once more and steps out of the airlock.

Unless Malcolm's goal has changed, he's still planning

on stealing the aft part of the *Slingshot*. And if so, he's still going to need to decouple it from the marketplace module. The problem is that Malcolm achieves his goal whether or not he decouples it the right way. And it would be so much faster and more efficient to simply blast the modules apart.

Jay can't see Malcolm, but he knows the other man has to be out here somewhere. At least Jay's connected back in with the others. Las routed their communications through this environment suit, which means that even though he's the only human within sight range, he's no longer alone.

"I'm scanning the surface," Ruby says. "No sign of Saint, but I do get some sort of weird energy signal near the connection point between Module E and the marketplace."

"Copy that."

Jay's spent plenty of time working in environment suits with his father, and as he pushes himself slowly along the surface of the *Slingshot*, he tells himself this is no different. But of course it is. Trip and fall on Corusca and you might bang a knee on a moon rock. Trip and lose your tether on the outside of a spacecraft in Durga's Belt and you'll spend your final hours drifting among the stars. Which probably isn't as peaceful a way to go as it sounds.

Slow and smooth is always faster, he reminds himself.

When he worked on the surface of Corusca with his father, he would look up into the sky to see their work illuminated by the glowing green, blue, and white orb of Indira. They would be repairing environment systems to make sure water kept being recycled and air kept flowing, that the millions of people living on Corusca could continue going about their daily lives without wondering where their next breath would come from. He'd felt pride, as a kid, in maintaining these feats of engineering so humanity could thrive beyond the limits of atmosphere and gravity.

But there had always been a voice in the back of his head wondering what the hell his ancestors had seen in the place. What brought his paternal great-grandparents from New Manila? What brought his maternal grandmother from New Sarjun? Why — when there was an option to *not* think about breathing — would you move someplace like Corusca?

Now, having spent the last three years navigating the even more precarious technological marvel that is life in Durga's Belt, Jay thinks he understands a little bit more. Sometimes you need to start from nothing if you want to build something truly incredible.

Why not build a space station out of hollowed-out stacked rocks and cover it with art? Why not create a giant ship that travels back and forth through the Belt with its cargo of fragile human lives and hope? Why not form a family on a cargo hauler that used to belong to a gangster? Why not step outside the crush of society's rules and petty fights and small cruelties and find your own way to survive?

An incoming connection request crackles through his thoughts. But it's not Ruby or Las. Jay frowns at the unknown ID appearing on his heads-up display and accepts the request.

"You're persistent, I'll give you that." Malcolm's voice is as intimate as if he were standing at Jay's shoulder. "I would have assumed you'd head right back to your ship as soon as you found out your friends were safe. Isn't that what you wanted?"

"What's your plan, Malcolm?" Jay turns to scan the area around him for any sign of the other man, finds nothing. "These people never did anything to you."

"You're right," Malcolm says. "But life is hard out here, isn't it? People have died for many worse reasons."

"And they've definitely died for better ones."

"Everyone on this ship had the opportunity to choose their fate, which isn't a luxury many people get out here.

They knew what refusing the cartel's protection meant. Now we need to make sure the rest of the Belt knows what that means, too."

"This isn't a message for the Pearls," Jay says. "You're puffing out your chest for everyone in the Belt."

He's come around the far side of the control unit and finally has a clear view of where Module E attaches to the marketplace. Malcolm isn't there, despite the unknown energy signature Ruby had noticed. Had he already planted a bomb? Jay turns, cursing the limited vision of the environment suit — and his swollen eye. He's a sitting target.

"Just the Belt?" Malcolm laughs. "By tomorrow there won't be a single person in the entire system who doesn't know the Maribi Cartel. Or the name Malcolm Saint."

"Yeah?"

"You'll never make it in time, Jay. You're still too far away."

Jay turns again, the back of his neck itching. He can't see Malcolm, but Malcolm can see him. Jay takes a deep breath and unhooks his tether — the time for slow and steady is over, and if Malcolm were going to shoot him outright, he would have done it already. It takes a moment to get used to the maneuvering thrusters on the unfamiliar environment suit, but Jay is soon skimming the surface on his way to the place where the modules attach.

"Is mass murder really the way you want to make a name for yourself?" he asks Malcolm. "You're hardly going to be remembered as a hero."

"You think I give a shit about that? My parents were patient. They waited their turn, they hoped for a change of luck — and they suffocated in the black. No one remembers their names, but no one will ever forget mine."

"Remembered as a lackey of the Maribi Cartel."

That sharp breath on the other side of the line, Jay's barbs have finally hit a nerve.

"Hardly for long," Malcolm growls. "And at least I'll be remembered. Good-bye, Jay."

Jay grabs for a handhold, jerking himself to a stop with a dull ache in his ribs that would probably be agonizing if it weren't for the emergency stims flooding his system. A projectile sparks off the surface of the *Slingshot* in front of him, right where his trajectory was about to take him.

It was close. Too close; Jay's environment suit starts blaring alarm bells again and his arm stiffens at the elbow as the suit automatically starts pumping sealant to fill the hole the projectile tore. Jay doesn't feel any pain in his arm, though — either nothing hit flesh or he's too pumped with meds to notice.

"He's at the recycler turret," Ruby says. "Behind you."

Jay flips to his back and fires at the human-shaped shadow behind the turret, one hand clutching his handhold. He fires again, but he can't move without turning his back on Malcolm.

"I can't get to the bomb," he says. "He's got me pinned down."

"I've got it," Lasadi says, and the *Nanshe* rises from behind the *Slingshot*.

The *Nanshe* doesn't have weapons that could pick a single person off the skin of the *Slingshot* without tearing through the ship itself, but Las can provide him cover. She eases the *Nanshe* between Jay and Malcolm, thrusters aimed in Malcolm's direction. Jay hears Malcolm's furious scream through the comms, but he doesn't wait to find out what happens next. He launches himself once more towards the connection point — and the out-of-place parcel blinking there.

The bomb's not big, but it doesn't have to be: Malcolm rigged it up on a bank of power cells on the aft end of the marketplace module, bonding it to the outermost cell with some sort of auto-weld cement that will take ages to chip through. Jay gets to his knees, unzipping the tool bag and fumbling for a laser cutter.

Thank the olds whoever maintains the *Slingshot* keeps things to code. Some of the repair jobs Jay's seen out here in the Belt have made his skin crawl, but the *Slingshot*'s power cells are attached by regulation-thickness tabs, set regulation-distance off from the surface of the ship. The laser cutter sputters, then flares to life along with the last spark of Jay's hope.

He can still get this. He still has time.

He slices carefully through the first tab, then the second, the third, finally cutting the fourth tab free with a sigh of relief. Jay shoves with all his might, shoulder wrenching; the power cell only shifts a few centimeters.

Something else is holding the cell in place.

Jay glances at the red light on Malcolm's bomb — is it his imagination, or is it blinking faster? — then pulls himself flat against the surface of the *Slingshot* to shine his light under the power cell. There's a nonregulation fifth connection point, barely out of easy reach. Jay wedges his torso between the power cell and its neighbor in order to reach the final tab, noting that the red light is definitely getting faster. He stretches the laser cutter in his hand out for a sloppy one-handed cut, and — there.

Jay braces himself against the power cell behind him and kicks with all his might. He's aiming for up, away from the *Slingshot*, though even just getting the bomb and its single power cell away from the rest of this bank will reduce the damage — maybe enough to save the ship.

The power cell drifts gently away.

Not nearly far enough.

"Jay," Las says through the comms. "Get out of there. I'll use the *Nanshe*'s grapple to pull it away."

"Not enough time," Jay says. He braces himself, mouth dry and heart racing. "Sorry, Las."

"No. Jay, don't — "

Jay unclips his tether and launches himself at the power cell, firing the environment suit's maneuvering thrusters at full blast. He wraps his arms around the cell, straining to keep hold as the thrusters send him and his deadly package farther out of range, the red light blinking rapidly in the corner of his eye.

Jay wrenches around to see the *Slingshot*, trying to gauge the distance. Are they far enough? They have to be, because the red light goes solid. Jay pushes himself away from the power cell with all his remaining strength, covering his head with his arms out of instinct; the gesture won't do anything to save him if he hasn't gotten far enough away.

A giant's hand crashes into his back.

The force flings him towards the *Slingshot*, but his relief is short-lived; his body skips across the surface like a stone across water. He scrambles for handholds, gloved fingers grasping for bolts and ridges in the metal plating and finding nothing, his stiff right arm brushing against the lip of an access hatch that his hand is too slow to close around, and before he can understand what has happened the ship is gone, his body tumbling and vision spiraling between stars and glimpses of the *Slingshot* — each glimpse taking him farther and farther away.

Someone's yelling for him, Lasadi calling his name. He screws his eyes shut, opens them to a chaos of spinning stars, and finally manages to answer. "I'm here."

Lasadi lets out a curse of relief. "You're where? I can't get a read on your suit. Tell me what you see."

"Hold on . . ." Jay blinks, trying to clear his vision, struggling to understand what he's seeing. He can't tell which direction he's spun off the *Slingshot* from. He's upside down one moment and right side up the next, each stolen sighting of the *Slingshot* smaller and smaller. His mind seems fuzzier, too. The spinning, the explosion? Are the stims wearing off? Or maybe his suit is feeding him something else. "Hold . . ."

Another woman's voice has joined Lasadi's. Ruby? Or — no. It's the automated voice from his environment suit. And the red lights smeared against the glittering black aren't the remnants of the bomb. His heads-up display is glaring warnings his vision is too blurred to read.

"Emergency mode activated," says his suit calmly. "Emergency mode activated. Initiating life support stasis."

"No," Jay says — thinks he says, because his tongue is already thick in his mouth by the time needles pierce his neck again. The terrifying red warnings gently fade to black.

CHAPTER 30
LASADI

Jay's voice goes static.

Lasadi lets her eyes close a moment, lets her mind clear. Lets panic and fear and worry drain from her body until she's as cold and empty as the void around them. If he was in one of the *Nanshe*'s environment suits she'd be able to track him, but now she has no bead on him, and if the *Slingshot*'s suits have emergency transponders for this type of situation, she's not able to pick up a signal.

But he's out there, and as of thirty seconds ago he's alive.

"Jay, come in. Jay. Come in."

Nothing from his channel but silence.

"Alex? Stay in your suit and be ready to take a walk. I'm patching external feeds down to you. We're looking for anything human."

Lasadi engages the *Nanshe*'s thrusters, brings the ship carefully alongside Module E of the *Slingshot*, then sets the autopilot to keep them in place while she scrolls through the *Nanshe*'s external cameras. She studies every jutting protrusion and discolored patch on the flat gray metal of the *Slingshot*'s exterior, trying to make out the form of a human body hiding on the surface of the ship. She's lost track of Malcolm Saint, too, but she doesn't give a shit about that. With any luck the *Nanshe*'s thrusters sent him on his own final journey into the starry expanse.

She spares a glance at the black scorches on the market-place module — the hull seems to have survived the blast — and when she's satisfied Jay's not still on the *Slingshot*, she turns her attention to the black.

Cold, unblinking stars fill her screen. Is this all Jay sees, too? Drifting into that glittering sea with his eyes wide and staring, trying to take comfort in the beauty while his hope fades that she'll find him? Though maybe he's been knocked unconscious. Or maybe he's facing back towards the *Slingshot*, drifting further out of her sight, unable to tell her where he is even while his own gaze is locked on the *Nanshe*.

Lasadi shoves those thoughts aside and stills her mind again. Start where he was last seen and work her way out from there, that's the plan. Study the footage in concentric circles, knowing Jay could be floating nearby — or could as easily have been thrown fast and far, tumbling and spinning in any direction.

"What do you see?" she asks Alex. "Anything?"

"Nothing yet, Cap."

"I'm taking us farther out."

One part of Lasadi's mind reminds her that a slow and methodical search will be more fruitful than fast and slip-shod, but another part of her mind is quietly performing calculations. The *Slingshot*'s environment suits are designed for quick repair jaunts, not long-term use. Jay hadn't gone out with an extra air tank, which means he has a maximum of an hour's air. More, if he's been knocked unconscious and isn't breathing so heavily. Less, if his suit suffered a puncture.

More than thirty minutes have passed since he left the airlock, and Lasadi still can't find him.

"I'm taking us farther out," she tells Alex again, painfully aware that every time they expand the circle of their search, they double the amount of glittering black they have to sift through for a humanoid speck. But this time, when Lasadi sets the autopilot and turns back to her screens, the *Nanshe* chimes a proximity alert. She calls the feed up like she has a dozen times before, her heart no less hopeful and her mind no less prepared for disappointment. Only now, the speck on her screen appears to be more than random debris.

She zooms in. It's a body; impossible at this distance to tell if it's Jay.

Lasadi flicks the feed down to the cargo bay, already maneuvering the *Nanshe* closer.

"Alex. Get prepped."

"It's him," Alex says, excitement in his voice.

It's a body, Lasadi thinks. But she doesn't correct Alex. Just because she's too terrified to be optimistic doesn't mean she needs to bring him down with her. Let him keep his hope for as long as he can — olds know they all need it. She opens up an all-frequency hail as they approach, gets no response. Whoever it is either isn't alive or has a problem with their comms. Lasadi tries again, gets nothing. But as the body slowly spins to face the *Nanshe*, she can tell one thing for sure.

They've found Jay.

His suit looks intact, but he's not moving. At this distance Lasadi can't tell if his eyes are open or closed.

"It's him," she says to Alex. "I'm coming alongside."

"Ready, Cap."

"Go ahead."

Lasadi holds their trajectory steady as the *Nanshe*

informs her Alex has opened up the airlock and is making his way outside the ship.

"What do you see?" she asks.

"His suit looks okay," Alex says. "But he's not responding. Either visually or over the comms."

"Understood." Lasadi tries to tell herself that doesn't mean anything. He could be unconscious. He could be stunned. He could have bled out in his suit during those slow, agonizing minutes he was waiting for her to find him, watching her look in all the wrong places while the world went dark. He could be —

"He's alive." Alex's voice is raspy with relief and excitement. "He's alive."

Lasadi takes a deep, shaky breath. "Secure him. Make sure you're both attached to the line."

"On it. We are both secured. Reeling in now."

Lasadi switches the *Nanshe* to autopilot once more and claws at the harness holding her to her chair. She makes it down to the cargo bay airlock by the time Alex reaches it from the outside, both his arms wrapped around Jay's chest despite being tethered together at the belt; he doesn't let go even once they're safely inside the *Nanshe*. She watches through the window as the outside airlock door irises shut, agonizingly slow. Watches the progress bar crawl as it repressurizes the chamber. Despite Alex's reassurances, Lasadi can't see anything in the glimpse she gets of Jay's face to tell her he's actually alive.

The airlock seal finally goes green and Lasadi slams her hand on the button to open the door. Alex floats out, Jay unmoving in his arms.

"The suit says it's stabilized his vitals," Alex says. "But he's hurt."

Lasadi nods and runs her fingers over the seal to Jay's helmet, folding it back into his suit with a hiss. His eyes are closed — one swollen shut — but he is breathing. And when she scans the suit for a readout of his vitals, the data comes back weak but stable.

"Help me get him to the medbay," Lasadi says, and together she and Alex float Jay up to the crew level, peel him out of his suit, strap him into the autodoc. Lasadi does her own estimation while the machine works: besides the swollen eye and the hastily bandaged gash on his bicep, he's got a few bruises blooming on his chest and a couple of needle clusters in his neck indicating his suit fed him more than one round of drugs. But his vital signs are steady and all the autodoc's scans are coming back clean.

"Hand me those shears," she tells Alex, and she gets to work on Jay's arm, cutting off the blood-soaked bandages so the autodoc can sterilize the wound and suture it up. Jay stays mercifully out until the wound is stitched and rebandaged, but then his eyelashes flutter open.

"Did it work?" he asks, voice hoarse; it's the sweetest sound she's heard in her life.

"You did it."

"What happened?"

Lasadi takes a sharp breath. "Like, what happened to you?"

"No, no." Jay waves a weary hand. "I remember everything fine. I mean, Malcolm. Escat. What happened."

"I lost track of Malcolm — so I'm hoping that means he's dead somewhere. Escat's safely sitting with his tail tucked between his legs back in his office. I wasn't really going to hand him over to the cartel for some vigilante justice."

"I know." Jay's good eye closes a long moment, flickers back open. "I trusted you."

"Thank you for that." Lasadi bends to kiss Jay on the brow above his undamaged eye. "Get some rest, hero. Time to go pick up the rest of the crew."

CHAPTER 31
RAJ

"WELL, THAT WAS SOMETHING," SAYS FIONA. SHE GLANCES over her shoulder at the door to the first-class lounge, skeptical eyebrow raised. "But at least we have it in writing."

Raj cracks his neck, shaking off the lounge's tacky luxury as much as the cloying insincerity of Escat's gratitude. "Thank you for saving the ship," he'd said, but he'd really been more concerned with saving his own ass.

Fortunately, his ass had been on this ship, which meant he'd been a willing player in their attempt to save it. Raj's last-minute addition to the plan had been simple and surprisingly effective: Get the two Maribi Cartel members off the shuttle, get Escat's aide to turn off the module's artificial gravity without warning, keep his own magboots turned on, shoot the cartel toughs with a stunner while they were floating in surprise. Top it off by sending a message to Malcolm Saint featuring Escat sitting in the shuttle in cuffs, and they were good to go.

Some plans don't need to be flashy.

The plan they've just hashed out between Escat and Fiona isn't flashy, either, but — as Fiona said — at least it's down in writing. Raj and Ruby had strongly hinted that if

Escat wanted to keep his involvement with the Maribi Cartel from leaking, he needed to install a citizen oversight committee to help with future decisions regarding governing the *Slingshot*. And they knew just the person to run that committee: the woman who already organized a mutual aid operation and was partly responsible for defusing the protest in the marketplace.

"I think it turned out well," Raj says.

"Not *that* well," says Alex; he and Lasadi, along with the crates that contain Karl Gatmaitan's belongings, are waiting for them in the corridor leading from the first-class lounge back to the marketplace. Returning the donations and handing Gatmaitan's property over for "investigation purposes" were part of the agreement with Escat. Alex waves a hand over the pile of crates. "I didn't get to steal any of this stuff."

"You got to shoot someone," Lasadi points out.

"With an electric barb."

Ruby shakes her head. "I'm sure the cap'll give you something stronger next time if you insist on being so useful." She takes charge of one of the crates, steering it down the corridor. "Speaking of being useful," she calls over her shoulder. "Let's get these loaded out."

Alex follows after Ruby, and Fiona claims one of the remaining crates. She pauses before she starts pushing, though, glancing between Raj and Lasadi. "He thinks you're Federation contraband task force agents, huh?"

"Raj and Ruby, at least," Lasadi says. "What I told you earlier is true. Vash and Gracie sent us to return Karl's belongings to them, and that's all we were here to do. Things just got a little complicated."

Fiona smiles. "Well, I'm glad you were here to help uncomplicate them."

"Same to you." But Lasadi's smile doesn't linger. "All the known cartel ships have left," she says, "and there's been no sign of Saint. But the Maribi Cartel isn't going to abandon their plans for taking control of the trade routes out here. You could be in danger."

Fiona shrugs and gives her crate a shove down the corridor. "I was already in danger. Malcolm Saint and I clashed more than once over the work I do with the community. I'd gone to Escat before to see if he would do anything about it, but he wouldn't. I always figured it was because he was in bed with the cartel. I was right."

Raj shoves a crate after her. "And he's not even getting a slap on the wrist for it." It eats at him, but he's not certain what they can do about it beyond putting measures in place to keep checks on him in the future. "The Federation's ignored complaints against him in the past."

"That was before they had another applicant for the job," Fiona says. "I know you said you'd make sure no one found out about his cartel connections if he worked with me, but I have my own evidence."

Raj grins. "And I would be delighted to make sure ours leaks to the right people."

"Really?" Fiona laughs. "Maybe some outsiders aren't so bad after all."

The marketplace is subdued today, as though everyone on the *Slingshot* is nursing a hangover from the live current of energy that had electrified them all yesterday. Or maybe people are simply spooked after the attempt to blow up the marketplace with them all in it, and have decided today is a great day to stay in their own bunks. Either way, Raj is relieved not to have to maneuver their cargo through a throng of bodies.

Fiona palms the panel on the stall next to hers — Karl Gatmaitan's old stall — and smiles when it opens for her. Another part of the agreement with Escat had been to give her that space to store donations to her mutual aid program, rent free.

Together, the crew work with Fiona to sort Gatmaitan's belongings from donations; in the end, there are only a few odd prototypes Raj thinks should be returned to Vash and Gracie, along with his notes. The rest they leave for Fiona to use how she can.

When they're finished, they gather outside the stall to survey their work.

"This is going to help so many people," says Fiona. "Thank you."

"You're the one helping," says Lasadi. "We were just in the right place at the right time."

"One more thing," Ruby says. She pulls the satchel she's been carrying off her shoulder and hands it to Fiona with a wink. "I've been playing around a bit with this contraption and I think I've got it working for real. It might still need some refining, but it's a start."

Fiona's eyes go wide as she pulls out the namidium detection device. "I thought you said this is fake."

"It *was* fake," Ruby says. "But I have a hard time letting puzzles go."

Raj shakes his head. "So that's what you were tinkering with all night."

"A girl's got to have hobbies," Ruby says breezily. "Obsessing over problems is mine. Drilling into asteroids all day, though? No, thank you. We'll never use it, and I figure Fiona can make sure the most people can benefit from it."

"Absolutely," Fiona says. "I will."

She leaves them all with good-bye hugs — even Raj — and then vanishes into Gatmaitan's old stall to continue her work.

"There are a lot of good ones out there still," Raj says as their little crew heads back to their berth. "But I'll be glad to be back on the *Nanshe*."

"Same," says Lasadi. She glances at Ruby. "Unless you

need more time to search for intel about your parents. Sorry things got so complicated so quickly."

"Always do with this crew." Ruby's expression has gone sober. "But I found time for that last night, too. My parents definitely booked passage on the *Slingshot*. As did the man who seemed to be hunting them."

"What?" Alex spins to face her, surprised. "Why didn't you tell me?"

"I only found out, didn't I," Ruby says with a wave of her hand; Raj barely catches the flash of hurt in Alex's eye before the kid turns away.

"Can you tell where they went next?" Raj asks.

The way Ruby's mouth flattens, the way she flicks her pinkie nail against her thumbnail — she does, and it's not good news.

"They sent an urgent message to a woman named Julieta Yang, saying they would come see her in Bulari. I looked her up, she still lives there."

"Bulari?" Raj lets out a sigh of relief. "Well, that's fine, then. You looked so upset, I thought you were going to say Arquelle — I'd have a tough time helping out in that case."

"I would never ask you all to come to Bulari," Ruby says.

"And we would never ask you to go by yourself," Lasadi answers. "Wherever you need to go for answers, we'll help you find them."

"Besides," Raj says, "I've always wanted to see New Sarjun."

"You're a horrible liar, love. No one's ever wanted to see New Sarjun." But the relief on Ruby's face is clear.

"It's actually true. Bulari sounds like an interesting city."

"You've a desperate yearning to experience heat rash and scorpion mites, have you."

Raj shrugs. "Bulari is supposed to have really good restaurants."

"And the highest murder rate per capita of anywhere in the Durga System."

"I actually think a couple of the hubs in Ironfall would take that distinction," Raj says. "And anyway, Bulari is one city. I think most of New Sarjun isn't that dangerous."

"Because the rest of the planet is uninhabitable, you mean."

"We'll just have to find out for ourselves," Lasadi says, palming open the *Nanshe*'s airlock and stepping back, arm out to welcome them all. Raj winks at her and follows Ruby in; the familiar scents and sounds of the cargo bay wrap around him like home.

CHAPTER 32
LASADI

LASADI'S ALWAYS HAPPY TO BE FLYING AGAIN, BUT TODAY MORE than ever. Though she hasn't been able to see the *Slingshot* in the *Nanshe*'s camera feeds for hours, she can still feel it like a physical presence at her back, fading a touch more with each minute of distance they put between them — and good riddance.

She's plotted a course back to the Traveler's Emporium; they'll stop there a week or so to unwind and recalibrate before heading off on their next adventure — to Bulari, apparently. Normally the thought of docking for so long would make Lasadi's skin crawl, but the Emporium had felt different than anywhere else she's been. She's actually looking forward to spending some more time with Raj's strange friends.

A rap on her door jostles her out of her thoughts, and her hand reaches automatically for the long-sleeved shirt she just pulled off. She stops herself. It'll be Raj, and he's already seen these scars. Multiple times, from about every angle imaginable — and he's seen so much more of her than the scars, too. She calls up the vid beside the door and goes still, heart suddenly pounding in her throat.

"Las, you got a sec?"

It's Jay; Lasadi's riveted with her hand on the door, trying to identify the emotion that has her frozen in place. It's not quite fear, though maybe that's where it started. But now she mostly feels exhausted, like an animal that's gotten so tired of running it's decided to stand its ground and fight instead.

Lasadi takes a deep breath and palms opens the door. "What's up?"

Jay's lips part in surprise, gaze dropping to her left shoulder, tracing the length of her arm and the slice of bare, scarred skin between the hem of her tank top and the top of her trousers. He clears his throat and meets her gaze once more. "I was going to ask if you wanted to keep me company while I make dinner."

"Yeah." Lasadi forces the word out and reaches for her shirt. "I'd love to. Let me grab — "

Before she can move, chattering voices from the cargo level below rise up the ladder into the crew quarters, and Ruby and Alex float into view. Ruby spots her first, eyes going wide; Alex turns to see what shocked his sister, trailing off midsentence. Lasadi's cheeks burn.

Alex breaks the silence. "Holy shit, Cap, no one ever told me you were *that* badass."

"Alex!" Ruby sounds horrified, but Lasadi can't help the laugh bubbling up through her chest.

"I've told you over and over how badass the captain is," Jay says, tossing Lasadi a wink and then turning to head back to the galley. "Not my fault you didn't listen."

And Lasadi's smile becomes real; she can't help it, with the way Alex is grinning at her.

"I just lived through a crash," she says to Alex. She grabs her shirt and pulls it on, but for once she doesn't bother buttoning it. It feels nice. Casual. She nods past him to Jay, who's pulling garlic and onions from the cupboard.

"That's the guy who pulled a gun on Nico Garnet's mercenaries' medic."

"She's too modest," Jay calls from the galley. "She's the one that piloted us out of a firefight while she was pinned to her seat with a piece of shrapnel the size of your arm."

Alex turns to stare at Jay. "You pulled a gun on Nico Garnet's mercenaries? By yourself?"

And like that, Jay's telling the story, and prompting Lasadi for her input; she ignores the nausea in her gut, the flashes of fire, the waves of memory crashing, because every time she feels like she's drowning she feels Raj's touch on her arm or catches Jay's smile or Ruby's "You good, Las?" or Alex's laugh of amazement.

The others go to bed after dinner, even Raj glancing between her and Jay and bidding them good night. Jay grabs a couple bulbs of beer and floats one her way. She follows him to the cargo bay where they can reminisce and share stories without bothering the others. An hour passes, more, before they finally drift into comfortable silence.

She's not sure what memories went tearing through Jay when he saw her scars; he hadn't seemed shocked. And now, when his gaze flicks to her collarbone, it dawns on her that she'd covered her scars in part because she assumed he would feel the same horrible flashbacks she did every time she looked in the mirror. At the beginning, she'd been trying to protect them both, to keep from reminding either of them of the horror of that day. But that kept them from sharing those good times, too. And she's not the only one who carries marks; continuing to hide hers did nothing but strengthen the barricade she'd slowly been building between them.

"I need to tell you something," Jay says after a long, comfortable pause. "I know our next priority is to figure out what happened to Ruby and Alex's parents, but I've been thinking about what happens after. And I have an idea you're not going to like."

"Let me tell you my bad idea first," Lasadi says. She'd bet anything they've been thinking the same thing. "We need to figure out what that Alliance Sabre was doing picking up illegal cargo in Durga's Belt. And then we need to stop them."

Jay breaks into a slow grin. "And how the hell would we do that?"

"We've got ourselves an Alliance deserter, a genius hacker, and a shockingly useful teen thief. We can probably come up with something."

"I bet we can." Jay throws his arm around her, pulling her close. "Night, Las. And thank you. For everything."

Raj's light is out when Lasadi finally heads back to her bunk, which is probably for the best. She feels like she could sleep for days, and with their course set and the *Nanshe*'s autopilot humming along, there's nothing to stop her. She slips into her bunk alone, but before she can close her eyes, a notification catches her attention. She has another new message from Tora Garnet.

URGENT. CALL ME, I HAVE SOMEONE YOU'LL WANT TO TALK TO.

Lasadi checks the time with a sinking feeling. It's after lunch in Ironfall, so Tora will definitely be up, and she won't be pleased if Lasadi keeps her waiting another full day by ignoring the message until Lasadi's morning. That, and something about the wording — "I have someone" — feels like a hidden blade.

What has Tora done?

Lasadi checks her image before putting through a video

call. She looks mostly presentable; when Tora answers, she's impeccable as always.

"Captain." Tora gives her a nod of respect that causes Lasadi to relax — at least slightly. They haven't spoken since she returned from Auburn Station. Tora had wanted Lasadi to continue working for her, but she hadn't seemed too upset when Lasadi refused. Of course, at the time, Tora was in the middle of leading a coup against her father. She'd been busy. It could be she's since reconsidered the decision to let Lasadi pay off the rest of her debts and take the *Nanshe*.

"I'm sorry I haven't gotten back to you," Lasadi says. "We've been busy."

"I'm glad you finally did." Something in Tora's tone sends a chill to the back of Lasadi's neck. Tora crooks a finger to someone offscreen and they step forward; Lasadi's heart stops.

"Evvi?" Lasadi's sister looks unharmed but exhausted, with dark circles under her eyes and a fierce expression on her face. Evvi doesn't answer; she's staring at Lasadi as though in shock. "Evvi, are you okay?" Lasadi leans in to the screen, furious. "We left on good terms, Tora. I don't know what your game is, but if you've hurt her — "

"She's a *guest*," Tora snaps. "Your sister showed up on *my* doorstep. Seems you haven't been responding to her messages either."

Evvi Faye finally seems to snap out of her trance, shaking her head. "I didn't quite believe it," she finally says. "When you didn't respond to my last message I thought it all must have been a cruel joke someone was playing on me. I started asking anyone I could find what they knew about the Battle of Tannis, and I kept hearing the name Nico Garnet. It was the only lead I had, so I came to Ironfall looking for him, and I found Tora. She has been a generous host."

"Evvi, you can't stay in Ironfall."

"And you have no right telling me what to do."

"Ironfall is dangerous."

"Then come save me." Evvi Faye fixes Lasadi with a final glare before she turns on her heel and stalks offscreen.

A long pause stretches between Lasadi and Tora before the other woman finally arches a perfect eyebrow. "And I thought Garnet family drama was bad," she says with a faint smile. "I'm keeping an eye on your sister — she won't find any trouble in Ironfall."

"Thank you." Evvi may be a sheltered young woman who knows nothing about life in the Pearls, but visiting Ironfall as a protected guest of the Garnet organization is probably as safe as she can get.

"Of course. And I do have a job for you, if you have a moment to see me. No rush, and no obligation." Tora leans forward to cut the feed. "Call me when you're in port, Captain. And I recommend you hurry. Your sister is welcome to stay my guest for as long as she likes, but I suspect her patience with you is much less generous than my own."

EPILOGUE: JAY

TODAY IT'S KAFUSA AGAIN, THE FAMILIAR BASS THRUM A SALVE on the sore muscles of Jay's torso, the intimate beat centering his mind. He's not really working, mostly tinkering and tidying in order to keep himself busy without straining his injuries too much.

When the chime comes announcing a visitor, Jay's alone in the *Nanshe*'s cargo bay. He calls up the feed to see who it is. Alex is in his bunk, Raj has gone on a grocery run, Ruby has grumped off on an errand that was "none of your business, is it," and Lasadi has gone to meet —

Her sister.

Jay'd caught a glimpse of Lasadi's sister once before, on the way to the *Slingshot* when he interrupted Lasadi while she still had her sister's vid call pulled up. The woman standing at the *Nanshe*'s cargo ramp is unmistakably Evora Faye Cazinho. Chestnut hair left free to curl around her pale cheeks and down her back, a nervous curiosity in her dark eyes, full lips parted as she turns her face to the *Nanshe*'s camera.

Jay wipes his hands on a rag and heads to the cargo bay door.

Lasadi's sister spins to face him when the door opens. She's standing at the bottom of the cargo ramp, a pair of bulky suitcases at her feet. Her dress is covered in sunny yellow flowers, with a sweetheart neckline and an impractical skirt that flows over the curve of her hips. Completely out of place in Ironfall's dockyard, but at least she's wearing practical boots and a sturdy canvas flight jacket.

She brushes a chestnut curl behind her ear, and Jay realizes he has no idea if Lasadi's hair is curly, too. They've fought together, bunked together, almost died together, and she always has it so tightly bound back in that braid.

"Hi, sorry, but I'm looking for the *Nanshe*?"

"You found it." Jay scans the dock; Lasadi's nowhere to be seen. So what is her sister doing here alone?

"Oh." She smiles. "I'm Evvi. Lasadi's sister."

"I know," Jay says. "She went to meet you."

"I thought I'd surprise her," Evvi says brightly. She takes a sharp breath. "And I didn't want her to surprise *me* by taking off and leaving me stranded. So I came here instead."

"She wouldn't — " Jay stops himself and allows Evvi a point with a nod. "She probably wouldn't do that."

"I told the server at the restaurant to wait ten minutes and then tell Lala where I'd gone. I didn't want her to worry. Too much."

"That's good." Old ones, but Lasadi is going to be furious.

"You're Jay, right?" Evvi had been looking over her shoulder, but now she turns her attention back to him — her full attention, and Jay suddenly wishes he was wearing something other than the tight, grease-stained Rhythm Machetes T-shirt and faded work pants that tend to ride too low on his hips. "Lala's told me about you."

"Has she?" What would Las have said about him? Jay

doesn't plan to ask out loud, but Evvi seems to see the question in his eyes.

"She has. She said you don't talk much, but you keep the universe running."

Jay's lips part, close again. He's not sure how to respond to the comment, or to the faint smile playing on Evvi's lips as she takes him in.

He clears his throat. "Can I help you with those bags?" he asks instead; he's expecting her to brush off his help like Lasadi would do, to insist on carrying the bulky cases herself. But Evvi seems relieved.

"I would appreciate that, thank you."

He descends the ramp and takes the first suitcase from her, marveling at the sparks flying between her soft fingers and his calloused, grease-imbued ones. *Ah, shit*, he thinks as she gives him a gorgeous, grateful smile that flips every switch down his spine.

"Happy to help," Jay says. "Welcome aboard the *Nanshe*."

❋

The adventure continues in the next book.

Get it at jessiekwak.com/nanshe.

DID YOU LIKE THE BOOK?

As a reader, I rely on book recommendations to help me pick what to read next.

As a writer, book recommendations are the most powerful way for me to get the word out to new readers.

If you liked this book, please leave a review on the platform of your choice — or tell a friend! It's the easiest way to help authors you enjoy keep producing great work.

Cheers!

Jessie

ABOUT JESSIE KWAK

Jessie Kwak has always lived in imaginary lands, from Arrakis and Ankh-Morpork to Earthsea, Tatooine, and now Portland, Oregon. As a writer, she sends readers on their own journeys to immersive worlds filled with fascinating characters, gunfights, explosions, and dinner parties.

When she's not raving about her latest favorite sci-fi series to her friends, she can be found sewing, mountain biking, or out exploring new worlds both at home and abroad.

(Author photo by Robert Kittilson.)

Connect with me:
www.jessiekwak.com
jessie@jessiekwak.com

facebook.com/JessieKwak

twitter.com/jkwak

instagram.com/kwakjessie

THE BULARI SAGA

With stakes this high, humanity doesn't need a hero. They need someone who can win.

Complete 5-book series + 3 prequel novellas + bonus short stories = over 500,000 words of adventure.

Willem Jaantzen didn't ask to be a hero. He just wants to keep his family safe in the shifting sands of Bulari's underground — and to get the city's upper crust to acknowledge just how far he's come since his days as an orphaned street kid. With his businesses thriving and his dark past swept into the annals of history, it looks like he has everything he could ever ask for. Until, that is, his oldest rival turns up murdered and the blame — and champagne — begins to flow.

It turns out Thala Coeur died as she lived: sowing chaos. And when a mysterious package bearing her call sign shows up on Jaantzen's doorstep, he and his family are quickly swallowed up in a web of lies, betrayals, and interplanetary politics. It'll only take one stray spark to start another civil war in the underworld, and Jaantzen's going to have to pull out every play from his notorious past if he wants to keep his city from going up in flames.

Jaantzen never wanted to be a hero, but that might just be a good thing. Because a hero could never stop the trouble that's heading humanity's way.

The Bulari Saga is a five-book series featuring gunfights, dinner parties, explosions, motorcycle chases, underworld intrigue, and a fiercely plucky found family who have each other's backs at every step. Perfect for fans of The Expanse, Firefly, and The Godfather.

Start the adventure today at jessiekwak.com/bulari-saga